MÁRCIO SOUZA was born in 1946 in Manaus, the Amazon region of Brazil. He began writing film criticism for newspapers when he was fourteen years old. He studied social sciences at the University of São Paulo. THE EMPEROR OF THE AMAZON, his first novel, was an extraordinary bestseller in Brazil and was serialized in a major Paris newspaper. Its pointed critique of Amazonian society cost him his job with the Ministry of Culture. In 1967 he published a collection of film writings under the title *O Mostrador de Sombras* (*Show of Shadows*). Souza is also a filmmaker and a dramatist. As a playwright, he works with Teatro Experimental do Sesc Amazonas, an important group fighting for the preservation and defense of the Amazon. His second novel MAD MARIA will be published by Avon/Bard Books in a translation by Thomas Colchie.

THE EMPEROR OF
THE AMAZON

MÁRCIO SOUZA

Translated by
THOMAS COLCHIE

 A BARD BOOK/PUBLISHED BY AVON BOOKS

THE EMPEROR OF THE AMAZON is an original publication of Avon Books. This work has never before appeared in book form in the English language.

Published in Brazil by Editora Civilização Brasileira, Rio de Janeiro.

AVON BOOKS
A division of
The Hearst Corporation
959 Eighth Avenue
New York, New York 10019

First Bard Printing, September, 1980
Second Printing

BARD IS A TRADEMARK OF THE HEARST CORPORATION
AND IS REGISTERED IN MANY COUNTRIES AROUND THE WORLD,
MARCA REGISTRADA, HECHO EN U.S.A.

Printed in the U.S.A.

THE LIFE & UNPRECEDENTED ADVEN-
TURES OF DOM LUIZ GALVEZ RODRIGUES
DE ARIA IN THE FABULOUS CITIES OF
THE AMAZON, INCLUDING A FARCICAL
CONQUEST OF THE TERRITORY OF ACRE,
SET FORTH WITH PERFECT EQUILIBRIUM
OF ARTISTRY & RATIOCINATION FOR
THE DELIGHT OF THE READER.

Beyond the equator, everything is permitted.
—Fifteenth-century Portuguese proverb

Not quite!
—Luiz Galvez, deposed

PART ONE

November 1897
to
November 1898

In the following episodes, language does not falter without the prior trip of intention. But if through carelessness or mischief I perhaps do pinch too hard, I have only to say to my censors what Bullfiddle, half-witted poet and farcical pedant from the Academy of Imitators, once replied when asked for the meaning of Deu de Deo. "You give what you got," he nimbly translated.

— Cervantes, EXEMPLARY NOVELS

Latifoliate Forest Primeval

This happens to be an adventure story where, in the end, the hero actually dies of old age in his bed. As for its style, the reader will undoubtedly complain that it smacks too much of the *art nouveau* of the '90s. But no matter, they just don't make adventure stories like they used to. Nowadays, exotic adventures and classical adjectives are completely out of fashion, not to mention the broad-leafed school of Parnassianism still extolled in the Amazonas of the early 1920s. And it is perhaps even possible to claim that this was the last exotic adventurer of them all, in the vast, dark Amazonian basin; an adventurer who actually witnessed those cigars being lit by one-hundred-dollar bills, confirming firsthand what legend later rekindled. After him? Multinational tourism.

Equatorial Fenimore Cooper

In 1945, an old Spaniard decided to write his memoirs. The fellow lived in Cádiz, was then retired, and had been tethered down for quite some time. Yet he had once loved to travel, and by his rare friends was taken for a consummate liar. In Spain, though, the lie has always held a certain savor . . . and in the Amazonas as well. The old man filled sheafs of pages with a whole series of extravagances, the same ones his friends were accustomed to listening to with such skepticism. He did not trouble himself about this, however, and knew that those very extravagances constituted the relevant facts of his life. A life, moreover, which was relevant only for having been spent in so irrelevant a place.

The old fellow died in 1946, and left no heirs. He had,

however, apparently already completed the memoir in question, because the entire bundle of papers, written in a firm, legible hand, was to be found some twenty years later, still in fair condition, enclosed in a cardboard portfolio. And like any good adventure story worthy of the name, it was finally discovered at one of those secondhand bookstores in Paris, by a Brazilian tourist, in 1973. How this manuscript left Cádiz and actually came to rest on the shelf of a *bouquiniste*, over on the Boulevard St. Michel, is still something of a mystery. What is certain is that the Brazilian, who was out rummaging through the antiquarian shops along the "Boule Miche," acquired the manuscript, which was drafted in Portuguese, for 350 francs, at the time not an outrageous sum. Rather a good buy even for an irrelevant manuscript. . . . Well, it took two days to read, and the Brazilian—thinking of the Romantic novelist José de Alencar, who had done something very similar with his *War of the Peddlers*—decided to edit and publish it. The Brazilian was none other than myself, and I confess to being rather taken with the extravagances of this nineteenth-century Spaniard. At any rate, from his yellowed stack of papers—discovered in such queer fashion, as Alencar himself might have said—I have patched together this narrative which is now being brought into print. And still harking back to my Alencar —our own, equatorial Cooper—let me likewise say to the reader: "Reconcile thyself to the world, which is but the Master Puppeteer of such playthings." As for myself, I hope to at least be able to recoup the 350 francs I spent on the manuscript, which was to have paid for, among other things, my bus trip to Nice and a dinner at Les Balcans.

Title Page

The ink is somewhat faded here and there, and the moths have tasted a few adjectives by now, but our story begins nonetheless, with reference to a triangle of territories that once belonged to the tribes of Amoaca, Arara, Canamari, and Ipuriná Indians. On the Bolivian maps of the period, it seems that this triangle was more or less

Terra Incognita, a zone of tropical diseases and sinuous rivers etched in between the adjacent frontiers of Bolivia, Peru, and Brazil. In sum, a place no Christian would ever choose to hang his hat. But a certain fellow from the state of Ceará, who had no hat, decided to leave his home in northern Brazil and make his way along the precipitous banks of a tortuous river, occasionally encountering some of those same Indians. Eventually, this Cearensian managed to erect an outpost. From there he wrote to the Viscount of Santo Elias, a very powerful merchant back in Belém, asking for some trading goods. The Ipuriná had informed the fellow that their river was called Aquiri. So the trader, with little patience for the art of calligraphy, simply scribbled this name on the envelope, which the viscount, after a devil of a time, guessed to be A-C-R-E. Thereupon, the viscount began to run an extremely lucrative business, from his office in the capital, without realizing that he had also baptized a territory. The Territory of Acre was rich in lovely specimens of *Hevea brasiliensis*, and would exist for many years under the sign of equivocation.

Postcard

1898, a July night in Belém, capital of Pará. I begin the tale of my life "in midvoyage," at the age of thirty-nine. From my memory arises a moon, spilling a tarnished glow on the water. The normally crowded popular market, Get-the-Best, is an empty silhouette, and at that late hour of the night the streets have finally become a little cooler. The houses, dark. . . . Electrified streetlamps attract hundreds of moths which flutter and fall to the ground, whirling gusts of confetti. From off the Bay of Guajará comes a soft breeze they call the Marajó, after an island of the same name. It allays the heat somewhat but also mingles the stench of tide with the musty odors of bilgewater. The whole area, which smells of pungent coumarin and tulipwood, is a particularly foul quarter of the city, full of rotten garbage and street muck. And the alleys offering access to the marketplace are precariously lit at best, so there is little movement along them at this hour. Only a few stragglers pass by, bohemians most likely, while I lie comfortably ensconced in a delightful little alcove. Or so it seemed . . .

Allegro Politico-Conjugal I

. . . because while I was so eagerly petting a certain perfumed body, down below on the street walked Luiz Trucco—better known as Dom Luiz—the for-the-moment solitary and quite disgusted official representative of Bolivia. It happened that Dom Luiz could no longer bear the monotony of those *fin de siècle* evenings in Belém. Personally, I did not share his negativity. For a number of years the rubber trade had offered an easy path to enrichment, and the Amazon had become something of an ideal testing ground. In this part of the world, the dissipation of acquired wealth was carried out with such prodigious ostentation that there was not enough imagination left to overcome its monotony. And so they turned to sin, for lack of imagination.

Luiz Trucco seemed to me to be a rather cosmopolitan fellow who simply was accustomed to the more varied offerings of cities like Milan and Buenos Aires, where he had previously served. For someone like him it must have grown tiresome to frequent the same cafés and inns, over and over, with always the same crowd of customers, a noisy, hurried clientele with little aptitude for genuine conversation. Trucco had therefore adopted the habit of indulging himself in endless walks, pursuing his rancor; and in the predawn hours of that early Sunday morning, shunning the habitual crowds, he had sought the tranquility of the fortress at the edge of the old city, where he might sit on the low stone wall overlooking the river. He may well have had reason to be pensive, but the play of light upon the water seemed a palliative to his woes. Yes, our Trucco was a very troubled fellow, occupying as he did an extremely sensitive post in the Bolivian diplomatic service.

Allegro Politico-Conjugal II

So while I was hungrily kissing a firm little breast, scented with piperioca, down below on the street went

Luiz Trucco, gripping the silver handle of his cedar cane. Heading home now, with his splendid cane taps resounding against the marble sidewalk. He seemed lost in thought, and precisely for that reason, unmindful of the three figures who followed him, as masked and sinister-looking as the entertainments of the period demanded. And of course, where else would these villains presume to waylay their victim but in the beshadowed doorway of the warehouse directly below, savagely encircling the old gentleman in his white linen suit, while he in turn began to deftly wield his cane like the baton of a veritable maestro. Yes, Trucco would have stoutly defended himself, no doubt; but he could not have survived for very long had not that damnable husband of the sweet Creole with whom I was busily fornicating at that precise moment burst into the room, surprising us both and wielding a thoroughly whetted broadsword, and had I not therefore leaped up and with a single bound gone sailing through the window, clutching the bare essentials of my discarded attire. In short, I was to land directly upon the four men who were scuffling down below, exactly as it should have occurred in any good serialized novel. Together, we instantly formed an amorphous ball on the ground, and I could hear my lovely Creole still howling upstairs, taking a sound thrashing from her Portuguese mariner of a husband. In the meantime, the three assailants were escaping around a corner, in the direction of the cathedral, while Trucco took to his heels in the opposite direction, leaving me floundering with my pants.

Allegro Politico-Conjugal III

Everything had happened so fast. I had heard all the commotion out there between them, but to be honest, I was involved with more important matters. What amazed me afterward was how Trucco had covered all that distance to the corner in so short a time, not to mention how I myself had escaped from that fall without a broken rib or something far worse. Anyway, I proceeded to walk over in Trucco's direction. He was standing in the lighted doorway of one of the cabarets, and now began to notice how barely dressed I was, in only my pants. Luckily I had managed to grab my jacket along with my pants. I was irremediably shoeless, but finally managed at least to buckle my belt and button up my jacket, while lamenting the handsome linen shirt I had been forced to leave behind. I felt comforted, though, to discover that my wallet with all my money—the little worldly wealth I had—was still in my pants pocket after all.

My Portrait

I already mentioned I was thirty-nine. Well, I was also tall, a bit lanky, and had a downy beard and pointy mustache. I wore rounded, gold-rimmed spectacles and had a slender, pointed nose. I am of Mediterranean extraction, so my skin was olive, and dark from the sun. I confess I was rather an attractive fellow. At the moment though, I noticed that Trucco was eyeing me incredulously. "Thanks for saving me from being assaulted in that way," he said to me, somewhat embarrassed at my appearance, which, we must agree, wasn't exactly the norm. I explained to him that I was hardly owed any thanks, that the entire incident had been nothing more than a series of mishaps, inevitable corollaries of an existence such as mine. I further elaborated that the one assaulted was in fact myself, by a husband armed with a broadsword; and then he told me his name (his own, that is): Luiz Trucco, Consul General to Brazil, from Bolivia. I responded by extending my hand and informing him that I myself was a journalist and my name was Galvez, Luiz Galvez. Trucco thanked me again, insisting I had gotten him out of a tight spot, and I could not convince him otherwise. He asked me if I would accept a drink with him, and we entered the busy cabaret. It was the Juno & Flora, offering as its nightly attraction the charms of one "Lili, the Invincible Armada," Cuban *actrice*, dancer *extraordinaire*, exquisite *contorsioniste* of tropical rhythms and Parnassian metrification.

Juno & Flora
Along with Other Mythological Divinities

The cabaret could hardly be called distinguished, but the ambience was generally warm and simple, and the place was well regarded for its long years of faithful service to its customers. A small establishment, it consisted of a number of sofas with rounded tables of grimy marble, dimly lit in the shadows. We took a table near the orchestra. The place was nearly empty, and only the most tenacious among its adepts were still hanging on. Two *femmes* were dancing a clumsy cancan, probably local girls, both of them sweating profusely. We were waited upon by Dona Flora, the peroxided, corpulent proprietress who could easily have been mistaken for a more mundane embodiment of the goddess Juno. We received her usual compliments, and Trucco ordered whiskey for the two of us. The music had already wound down to that end-of-the-evening crawl when the waiter brought us our drinks. Trucco asked him if Lili was going to come on again that night, but the waiter told him curtly that her last number was always shortly after midnight. The place bred a definite air of familiarity, and two sirens came over to sit at our table. I pulled up a couple of chairs for them and noticed that they were somewhat elderly and rather the worse for wear, so I decided to just sit back and watch the world go by, while Trucco tried to exchange a few amenities with first one and then the other.

An Uneasy Bolivian

Trucco seemed ill disposed to his conversation with the two *cocottes*. He informed me a little later that he couldn't understand why such types were even allowed to enter places like that. Not that he was becoming a prude, mind you, but simply that he had grown more solitary of late, and the experience of such a mercenary solicitude as that of our two sirens left him irritated. The truth, however, was that Trucco could barely control his nerves, believing there was some sort of conspiracy underway aimed at his person or his country. In fact, whatever Brazilians did, Trucco took to be an insult, and the ostentatiousness of it all left him rather uneasy. He realized that he was getting on in years, and that the little time he had left would hardly be sufficient for what still needed to be accomplished.

Dialogue in the Juno and Flora

GALVEZ: Very exclusive place, eh?

TRUCCO: A lousy backwater dump. . . .

GALVEZ: To me it's paradise.

TRUCCO: Think the girls want a drink?

GALVEZ (in a loud voice): Want something to drink?

FIRST *COCOTTE: Oui, mon copain.* . . .

SECOND *COCOTTE:* But *uv course*, some champagne, no?

TRUCCO: A bottle of Veuve Cliquot, make it a '55.

GALVEZ: *Madre de Dios!*

TRUCCO: Out here, history is made in the bordello.

GALVEZ: Sacred history, to be sure. . . .

TRUCCO: Yes, of rich swines and cheap politicians.

GALVEZ: So what's so bad about that?

TRUCCO: We'll all be forgotten, that's what, and so will they. Even as libertines. . . .

GALVEZ: Here's to Bolivia!

TRUCCO: To Bolivia! No one will remember anything.

GALVEZ: What about the photograph?

TRUCCO: Black and white. . . . My face came out so white, I look like I'm wearing powder.

SECOND *COCOTTE:* Oh, I 'ave such an eetch *dans la twatte!*

Mythologies

The chorus girls, meanwhile, were attacking their high-step with a vengeance, kicking their legs out to almost the tip of my nose. I could even say that I caught the definite odor of feminine transpiration, and the two *femmes* showed no timidity about hiking up their skirts or lifting legs before so many respectable gentlemen, yet quite surpassed Queen Victoria herself in their utter disdain for underwear. So there amid the all-pervasive stench of stale cigar smoke—to gargles of raucous laughter and cries of "Shake them tails, you honeys"—the chorus girls continued to bounce to and fro, and I confess that it was not unlike being set upon by some wrathful woodland deities. One such slut was shuddering over a series of licks on her arm, the source of which was a quinquegenarian fop out of a Goncourt brothers novel, with a tongue the size of a cow's. He was a shriveled specimen, to be sure, prematurely aged from the rigors of the rubber trade. On another sofa, a Valkyrie out of a nightmare straddled the leg of a young dandy, shouting obscenities along with absurdities the likes of "Oh, my boy, my innocent babe!" And a dark-skinned, full-lipped Bacchus, with a scar upon his face, was busy pouring wine into the milky cleavage of his succulent companion.

I began to think Trucco was right to an extent, to feel so irritated by all this vulgarity and dreams of belated chastity. Hands, arms, legs, muslin, expensive cashmere and cheap calicos, all entertwining in prolonged nocturnal pollutions. And I could safely swear they were definitely out of step with the beat of the Viennese polka, moving to a different musical cadence—more *andante* than *allegro*. Then a bloated-looking stag suddenly collapsed across a table, sending bottles and glasses flying, and likewise spilling his female companion; after which a pair of oxen proceeded to carry him out bodily, without neglecting to administer a healthy drubbing in the process. And all with the utmost tranquility, not a protest or a whimper, not the slightest alteration of expression, save on the face of the waiter, forced to pick up the broken shards of glass from the carpeted floor.

Trucco was already quite drunk and seemed to be the only one who was threatened by the whole scene. Until finally I comprehended the truth of that suspect disgust which had lately taken such a hold on my companion: it was envy, envy for the vitality of life in that half-light full of cigar-smoking upstarts comfortably ensconced between a full bottle and an easy whore. Trucco refused to accept the fact that he had arrived a little too late in life to partake of this banquet of debauched satisfactions. After all, such cabarets provided the perfect escape for these rubber barons from the inordinate loneliness of that virginal jungle which I had yet to experience myself but could well imagine in its harshness and solitude. Trucco was obviously plastered, and I began to feel irritated as well, besides which, the two *cocottes* were constantly reaching for my crotch, while clawing at the back of my neck with those long talons.

The Ethics of Spinoza

In the midst of all the odors of sweated clothes and spent perfumes, Senator Hipólito Moriera was lifting a skirt draped over the as yet unvegetated pubis of his little fifteen-year-old cousin. She giggled and crossed her legs, which the beringed fingers of the insistent senator were busy fondling. The giggle, coupled with the gesture, temporarily outflanked the preliminary sortie of old Hipólito, who began scratching his beard while threads of saliva were dripping from a corner of his mouth. The old rascal was hungry for the prize, but was letting himself be blown off course by the stealth and seeming modesty of the girl in question. Senator Hipólito, bulwark of society, was finally triumphant, however, as with trembling fingers he boarded her besieged vessel. Happy old pirate. . . .

The Restless and Drunken Bolivian

Never drink with a Bolivian! Trucco had finally decided to confide to me the true substance of his anger. He muttered in my ear that Bolivia was also entitled to sup at such tables, which only the wealth of rubber apparently afforded. I tapped the *cocotte* nearest to me on the shoulder and stood up.

Watercolor

It was daybreak. . . .

The light above Belém was hardly made for bohemian eyes. We went out onto the street, where servants and peddlers were already running about with baskets on their heads. We set out to cross the old quarter of the city, whose houses were awakening in exhaustion from a night which still seemed victorious. Trucco was stumbling along with the help of my legs, while our two *cocottes* followed closely behind like a pair of household pets. Yet they were happy enough, and no one seemed terribly shocked at our general appearance, passing us by indifferently. A private in the civil guard, leaning on an iron lamp post, scratched his privates with accomplished dexterity. Another peaceful day. . . .

Playing Handle to an Umbrella

TRUCCO: This looks like Lisbon. Ever been to Lisbon?

GALVEZ: Yes, I know Lisbon quite well, a beautiful city.

TRUCCO: Even the *stench* of Belém reminds me of Portugal.

GALVEZ: La Paz must stink like Madrid, eh?

TRUCCO: It's just that I have no patience for vulgarity.

GALVEZ: The girls still seem to be following us.

TRUCCO: Get rid of them. Here, give them this.

GALVEZ: Your wish is my command.

Finances

I gave the two sirens the money and put Trucco into a cabriolet. The old man thanked me, gestured vaguely to the coachman, and sank back into the carriage. I still preferred to walk a bit, but the two *cocottes* had little to say; they were busy counting and recounting the money from Trucco, until I began to fear that they might want even more. I was so short myself at the moment that I had already contemplated asking for an advance over at the paper, a little later in the day. Trucco must have awakened with one hell of a hangover.

To the Dining Room

Trucco had made up his mind to include me among his reduced list of friends; for some reason he had taken a liking to my face, I suppose. I arrived at seven, and a very stuffy butler received me at the door. Trucco was obviously living quite comfortably, this time looking clean-shaven and well rested. He even seemed a bit younger to me. The butler was adding the finishing touches to the table for four, while a pair of maids tooks turns setting out the china. In the meantime, Trucco invited me to come have a look at his collection of firearms. Old pistols arranged on shelves of dark wood and protected in velvet-lined boxes with glass lids. He described each weapon with great affection, the bore, the types of metal, some tooled in gold. A collection demonstrating a healthy His-panic passion for violence. I was finally even slightly moved by Luiz Trucco, but did not allow that to be taken for complicity.

A Couple Arrives

A gong rang and Trucco placed a Spanish pistol back into its case. The other two guests had arrived, a well-to-do couple of the *haute bourgeoisie* there in Pará. I was intro-duced to Cira and Alberto Chermont de Albuquerque. She had a childlike body and was wearing a simple, straight-cut dress of white linen. I recall the detail because the encounter was certainly the most notable I think I had in Belém. Cira looked to be about twenty, with gray eyes and a crimson, half-mocking smile. Alberto was a pros-perous dealer in lumber, from a traditional Paraensian family. He was short and energetic-looking, but with a delicate voice, and always kept his face quite cleanly shaven. I know that he felt more patience than love for his wife, and often came to mind as an example of the stoic victim in one of those marriages of convenience. He wore a dark dinner jacket, and his cufflinks were made of Peruvian silver *libras*.

Cira had attended a religious school for girls, in Belgium, and then studied law in São Paulo. Alberto's *vita* was more mundane, limited to a business course in Recife and a nose for nuances in the wood market. His wife, however, who knew herself to be rich, elegant, and beautiful, had cultivated a habit of shocking the provincial mentality. For other women less favored by intelligence and good fortune, Cira's life-style provided fertile ground for envious gossip and muted self-reproach. None of which prevented Cira from still setting the parameters of fashionable-woman, touched-by-notoriety.

Cira and Alberto were smiling to one another at our first encounter, but she seemed rather to eclipse him with her dominant air of self-assuredness. Trucco presented me as a journalist from the *Pará Provincial*, and I heard Cira confess to be one of the newspaper's readers, but one who sorely lamented the little importance given to international news. We were then served a pleasant-tasting liqueur.

Encyclopedia Britannica

Hevea brasiliensis is a plant species of the family Euphorbiaciae, and will always play a part in my story similar to the wings of a stage for the scene of a comedy. It is the principal source for the extraction of latex. Fully grown, it measures approximately thirty meters in height, with a trunk of about three meters around. A lovely-looking tree, there is no doubt, and whenever I was able to recognize one of these specimens in the middle of the jungle, I never failed to render homage. The leaves are of a dark-green color and smooth to the touch. Within the trunk flows a white sap: the latex. Solidified latex becomes rubber. Botanists have yet to understand fully the function of the latex in the metabolic process of the tree—a question of little import, however, now that merchants and traders have promulgated a sufficient number of nonbotanical reasons for the existence of the same. It is interesting to note, in passing, that *Hevea brasiliensis* happens to be hermaphroditic.

Our Scenario

The liqueur which Trucco served us had been produced right here in Belém, by a German agronomist who had made a fortune selling produce to the merchants of latex. Trucco was renting the house he inhabited from Dr. Eugênio Bentes Ferreira, a general practitioner who had accumulated his riches by treating the sicknesses of those same merchants of latex. In fact, the wealth of quite a few people in Belém, during this period, may be said to have been derived in some manner from the trade in latex, and Trucco's present abode attested to the fact in all its splendor. A lofty-windowed palazzo, an enormous dining room, its parquet flooring of Scotch pine in alternating patterns of dark and light. And on the walls, whole murals of operatic scenes, set off by an eighteenth-century chandelier, while several windows offered breathtaking views of a florid garden, with its English cast-iron fountain. We were seated in wicker chairs, and a curious-looking Chinese vase served as the centerpiece for the table.

Dinner Menu at Luiz Trucco's

Entrées.
Bouillabaisse.
Stuffed spiced crabs on the half shell.
Duck in manioc-and-pepper sauce.
Quiche à la Dona Isabel de Vilhena.
White wine.
Turkish coffee.
Trujillo cigars.

Good Food and Conversation

Dona Conceição Ferreira Belmonte, widow of General Belmonte and affluent proprietress of the overseas shipping firm of Ferreira, Salgado & Company, had lately returned from a voyage to Portugal, completely enamored of the cultivation of roses. She therefore initiated the construction of an awesome greenhouse and proceeded to cultivate her tiny seedlings. The latter a present from the curate of Portimão, in whose presence she had passed a summer of indolence, sun, and prayer. Two months later, however, suffering from an acute asthmatic seizure—and under the tutelage of an obscure healer from Ananindeua —she ordered the roses replaced with papayas and the useless greenhouse totally dismantled. . . .

The colonel of the civil guard, Apolidório Tristão de Magalhães, was one of Belém's more fervent aspirants to the condition of writer, and the owner of an immense library (practically untouched, given his inability to make out even the simplest label on a bottle of tonic). He was also apparently in possession of a rather odd souvenir which he nonetheless revered as a holy relic: a pair of undershorts belonging to the prodigious Henrique Maximiliano Coelho Neto, author of voluminous works of prose (120 vols. at his death), symphonically orchestrated by a twenty-thousand word vocabulary. Colonel Tristão, however, had learned to sign his name only at the age of fifty, when finally obliged to register his holdings on the Isle of Laguna, a vast feudal property several kilometers from the town of Melgaço. Still, he had somehow managed to monopolize the great writer during the latter's stay in Belém: lodging, entertaining, and lionizing him, not to mention posing at his side in countless photographs taken for posterity. Then finally—taking advantage of a propitious moment of grand, authorly distraction—Colonel Tristão had pinched, as it were, the intimate apparel in question, which now adorned the wall of his library, silver-framed, in a position of prominence and veneration. . . .

The duck was delicious, the wine superb. The subjects of conversation were appropriate enough for those who adore the extravagances of the typical *nouveaux riches*. As for myself, I was content to observe the irony of Cira, in that coloratura-soprano voice of hers with its enviable intonation of self-assurance. I chose not to smoke the cigars. . . .

Imperialistic Tremors

Coelho Neto's undershorts were still giving us a chuckle when the gong for the door sounded a second time, and a man with a jovial air and a blue scarf tied around his neck entered with modest apologies for his unexpected arrival. It was Michael Kennedy, Consul General to Brazil from the United States, stationed in Belém. A typical American bureaucrat who specialized in provoking chills. Girls of a marriageable age would tremble over his ready bachelorhood and Irish Catholic features. Merchants and politicians shook in the face of his machinations and promises; and patriots shivered at the continual threats his country was wont to bandy against the integrity of the Amazon. Yet I felt quite positive that Kennedy himself had never experienced the least mercurial tremor, but rather seemed wholly accustomed to making his way through Belém as a surgeon would through the entrails of a patient. Kennedy was competent, discreet, and precise. It ought to be obvious, moreover, that I could never sympathize with such a fellow. At the moment, he was in possession of a blue envelope, which he immediately handed to Trucco. Trucco opened it hastily, then perused its contents carefully. I think that he actually read the text more than once, and each time his eyes went over the page, it seemed to relieve him of a tremendous burden. Until finally, he looked up at all of us and, while he proceeded to fold up the paper, began telling us that Bolivia was now negotiating with the United States to find a solution to the problem of Acre. It was the first time that I had my attention drawn to the question posed by Acre, given that Americans are not known for their interest in mere trifles. Cira was trembling slightly, and her case seemed to be of the patriotic variety.

Acrean Equivocations

The right of Bolivia to the territories of Acre had been recognized in 1867, by the Treaty of Ayacucho. But Article II of that treaty had also established for Brazilians the *uti possideţis* thereof. The borders of Acre had yet to be determined, and it was only in 1895 that the two governments actually commenced negotiations in this respect. Since 1877, however, Acre has been virtually occupied by settlers from Ceará.

The Politics of Dessert

Trucco was so cheered by the sudden news that he started babbling about plans of a Bolivia allied to the United States. Cira now exhibited a vibrant curiosity, coupled with an attitude of hostility toward the facts themselves. And I listened as Trucco, with no qualms whatsoever, hopelessly confirmed Kennedy's opinion of Latin Americans: a people of questionable statecraft and lamentable business acumen. Needless to say, he was visibly annoyed with Trucco's lack of discretion. I confess that I was somewhat perplexed by Cira's attitude, yet she rekindled my appetite for the unexpected—even if, for the moment, the feeling was still ambiguous, and could hardly have passed for more than a vague interest in her personally: as a woman. The butler began to serve a delicious Chambertin—to commemorate, obviously. I recalled that the last time I'd had a Chambertin had been back in Buenos Aires.

Literary Reflections

A hot August, in 1898. I was plodding through the insufferable round of day-to-day activities. Forgive me, but daily routine does exist, even in the best of adventures, and mine was no exception. I left the office of the paper and gazed out upon the late afternoon with its affected glow that, to my knowledge, still inspired no Parnassian sonnets. The reader is perhaps curious to know if there was some mystery afoot in this Amazonian metropolis. I answer that there was, but a mystery difficult to comprehend. And I was, for the moment, more interested in acquainting myself with life in the province, when I wasn't overtaken with a melancholy longing for the old days in

San Sebastián, or those more recent, nightly carousals at
the Juno & Flora. I had heard "Lili, the Invincible Armada,"
but was disappointed by her too androgynous aspect—a
petite woman, fragile and pale, with nearly no breasts to
her; who danced like some mannered El Greco angel. My
travels and my flights of fancy helped to sustain me, and so
did Cira's face, restless with curiosity. I was attracted, I
admit, to that fountain of feminine impetuosity, in a land
where women were too muted even to moan in bed.

The river always seemed empty; in the distance, only a
few sad-looking fishing boats with grimy, Moorish sails. . . .
How different the beaches of Biscaya, or the tree-lined
Avenida Farest in Buenos Aires. . . . And what of the cool
corridors of the Spanish Chancellory in Paris? Or Rome,
with its fountains of dripping tritons? Ah, those muddy
skies of Biscaya, and all the women I once loved: threads
of blood, silk, and sand—hymens! Lifting their skirts to
compel my attention—so many layers of petticoat—tight-
ening their hips and strutting about, then with pouted lips
and lowered eyelashes, bending over thighs sheathed in
silk stockings to unbuckle a brocaded shoe. Boots and
shoes now gloriously visible (after years of hoopskirts!) to
my unbridled fetishism . . .

Fatherly Advice

My father had warned me, "Life is little more than
sculpting one's death out of the end of each day, knowing
it to be numbered among the last, of the last year in the
last decade." The sunlight on my bedroom window curtain. . . . Small compensatory satisfaction of a soft bed
amid the dust of a vast colonial empire in its final days of
disintegration and collapse. Cuba, and morning coffee at
the office of the Spanish diplomatic legation. Anarchists;
and Americans grimy with dust, clumsily staining the
carpets of the Governor of Havana. The yellow waters of
the Rio Amazonas; and my family of military *hidalgos*.
My own father, a man of traditional obligations, watching
the lights of the century grow dim; spyglass in hand, bark-
ing orders from under his mustachio, the Admiral of
Cádiz, blown by every bureaucratic wind, and outraged at

the becalmed ruin of the Spanish fleet. Yet I also came to merit this life through my mother, a Spanish woman from Tangiers.

Rain Forest

I no longer had that palazzo in Cádiz, refuge of stone echoing with conversation and laughter, where so much of the family's time was spent together, out on the terrace overlooking the sea. Now, in the belly of the Amazon, I lacked any motive for such routines and sought to flee the text of the drama. Being a profound believer in life's *coups de main* (Cira's expression) . . .

The Café Abolition

There was a fine drizzle coming down on that late afternoon, so I ran into the Café Abolition, only place in the world where they serve you manioc meal with your *jerez*. I took a corner table and ended up meditating upon the comedy called life, something anyone tends to do when idling away the time or simply without a razor at the throat. Then a carriage stopped and its coachman came in to deliver a message from Cira. So I entered that refuge of soft leather, shutting the little carriage door behind me, and sat back, calmly gazing at her as we rolled through the cobblestone streets. She broke one spell with another by suddenly kissing me, and I did not fail to appreciate the extravagance of the gesture. Outside: that fine, humid, fortunate drizzle. It looked as if I had finally arranged a mistress for myself.

An Invitation

Trucco informed me that we were invited to attend the birthday party of the mayor's wife. It was on a Thursday, and I accepted the invitation, certain that it would turn out to be quite amusing. I almost walked in with the entourage of the governor himself, Paes de Carvalho. I was eager to meet Dona Irene (whose birthday it was), a species of folkloric myth among Paraensian society.

THE EMPEROR OF THE AMAZON

Antecedent to the Party

Two days before the party, a decorated cake had been ordered from a confectioner named Domenico Lizzano, ex-railwayman from Turin, who had made his fortune preparing choice delicacies to garnish the tables of the merchants of latex. Lizzano was preparing, besides the order for Dona Irene, another equally monumental edifice. The cakes were of the same size and pattern, but different in color. The pink one was for Colonel Vicente Telles de Teixeira Mendes, infamous sybarite and diligent subscriber to *Punch* magazine. Also a frequent passenger on the S.S. *Raethia*, Colonel Teixeira Mendes was, to give him his proper due, the spiritual founder of this particular mold of confection, circular in shape, deeply layered, and housing a "Surprise!" in its midst. The "Surprise!" in question was always a seminude chorus girl who would spring forth at a predetermined moment and further fuel the already scandalous private receptions of the colonel. The blue one with the forty-eight candles, for Dona Irene, was offspring of the various distortions that the colonel's contribution to the history of ideas had already suffered in Belém. It had, for instance, no "Surprise!" inside, and was therefore dutifully stuffed with confections.

European Upbringing

I have already mentioned that Dona Irene was something of a legend in the domestic folklore of Belém. Arising from rather humble origins, she had nevertheless managed to steal the heart of the future mayor with her ample buttocks, her tremendous vivacity, and the sizable impact of more than a hundred kilos of unadulterated passion. She would make consistently valiant efforts to guard against the imperfections wrought by a poverty-stricken childhood, but the results were almost always disastrous. Yet she was a necessary creature to Paraensian society, providing a welcome yardstick to their own good manners. A simple woman and daughter of the Rio Madeira, she had married the mayor when he was still a young law student. The marriage was secret, and the family— to avoid a scandal—summarily shipped the two lovers to Rio de Janeiro, where for three years Dona Irene was kept a virtual prisoner, in the care of a French tutor and a German governess. What emerged was this wholly ingenuous force of nature who smelled of patchouli and thought that Halley's comet was an act in the circus. She collected rare cheeses, however; the private passion of her governess from Potsdam.

Puppet Theater

I have always believed that the ridiculous can be of interest when practiced with candor, and that garrulous wife of the mayor, who had just received the governor himself with complete intimacy, was certainly capable of provoking lapses of etiquette worthy of the utmost candor. Clearly, Dona Irene had immediately won my sympathy. In Belém, people stuffed themselves with formalities, resorting to good breeding as a species of legal restraint upon their own excesses. Yet her house was full, and I noted that the ceiling was decorated with romantic clouds in strong brush strokes and cherubs gamboling across a Prussian-blue sky. You would imagine that the little cherubs, apparently so innocent, were drinking tall glasses of foaming beer, and I silently toasted the cynicism of the artist.

Cira was wearing an elegant green silk dress, and I immediately forgot the inebriation of angels. She was pretending interest in her husband's conversation (which undoubtedly concerned hardwoods) with the gentleman in the sleek mustache exuding an Earl of Chesterfield manner about his person. A living anachronism amid the murmurs of festivity. . . . I began to think about the power which money wields, and it was precisely here that I could duly appreciate this. Of course, I'd always been in the presence of power; after all, I'd been a diplomat, and had therefore mingled with the elite and their manias. But in Europe, power was more of a natural consequence; one did not dwell upon the presence of money any more than one

31

would ask about the quality of a wine, or its value. Wine was wine, and always of quality. Money was the same sort of daily wine, an intimate apparel and an inner soul, a metaphysics. In Belém, however, money was in no sense metaphysical, it was there—and I could ascertain its palpable dimensions in the huge rose birthday cake, in the silver serving trays, in the lavish jewels adorning the necks of all the ladies. The very torso of money displayed itself naked, glibly instructing the maid who served the punch. In fact, I could even say that money was literally on the tip of every tongue. Ambiguous offspring of new-found wealth, promiscuous inhabitants of a primitive land, these people had yet to shed their ostentation or suitably clothe their economic prowess. It was this ambivalence which Trucco, in his frustration, failed to comprehend and thereby confused with vulgarity. But out in the frontiers of the world there is no such thing as vulgarity. A Parisian can be vulgar, something which Dona Irene could never achieve, no matter how many *gaffes* or *faux pas* she might hazard to commit.

Aphorism on Ostentation

I learned that the *parvenu* is only disagreeable to the extent that he amplifies the details of human misery.

Trucco the Misanthrope

The consul general from Bolivia was spinning a few mercenary circumlocutions around the double wedding ring on the fourth finger, left hand, of a widow busy dissembling her long look of winter. The widow kept a bank account in Switzerland. Trucco's salary usually arrived one month late.

Mischief I

The gentlemen had formed a semicircle directly behind the chairs where the ladies were seated, and Dona Eudóxia Vasconcelos Negreiros was deftly executing a waltz.

Waltzes, of course, were civilization itself, and the thin cambric blouse of Dona Eudóxia rose and fell with the hearts of her audience. A marvel of rhythm, considering the cold technique of the pianist. Dona Eudóxia found in everything motives for condemnation, well enough I knew. I had had the good fortune to befriend a former student of hers, a creature with no inclination for the piano, who had nevertheless managed to wreck Dona Eudóxia's marriage, thereby liberating the latter's husband from the matrimonial holocaust to which he had consigned himself. It seems that while Dona Eudóxia was busily waging one of her annual campaigns to eradicate *carimbó* dancing among the populace during Candlelight-Nazareth processions, Amethista (the pupil without any vocation) was practicing a singular brand of solmization (far from her exercises in Boccherini minuets and Chopin nocturnes) in the amorous ear of the adulterer.

Surprise!

Dona Irene blew out the forty-eight candles on the rose cake, and we applauded. But hardly had she touched the frosting with a knife when the Tower of Babel shook to its foundations, as if the judgment of the Lord were at hand. The entire confection exploded like a volcano and bits of icing streamed in all directions, while a scantily clad chorus girl leaped out onto the table, unfolding her lovely form on the spot, and deftly intoning the following invitation:

> "Whoever wants to taste my grapes,
> Whoever wants to try his luck,
> Come pick but, *pleqse*, don't squeeze!
> You see, these grapes are made to suck. . . ."

A Swoonful of Proper Etiquette

An infantile rhyme, no doubt, but of extraordinary effect. The chorus girl had hardly commenced her lyric when Dona Irene had the good sense to faint dead away into the arms of her husband. The other ladies fled the salon, and really no one was left to help the mayor out of his predicament—red-faced and panting, I don't know whether from horror or the sheer weight of his conjugal burden. The chorus girl, meantime, immediately gathered that this was no place to suck grapes and grabbed the lid of the cake to try to cover herself. She then attempted to leap from the table, but the frosting that covered the sole of her shoe caused her to slide in the direction of the governor. Paes de Carvalho, in turn, fell against a console table but, in order not to smash a vase, embraced the chorus girl and tumbled to the floor himself, his body fully extended. The landing was such that the chorus girl escaped unharmed and Paes de Carvalho had to be carried away, unconscious, by two partisans from his entourage. The party had definitely ended, and we left there without knowing for sure whether Dona Irene had ordered the "Surprise!" or if there had been some sort of mixup. . . . It was, of course, the latter.

Proof of the Mistake

It was learned by my paper that, at the same moment at which the chorus girl was inciting Dona Irene's guests to suck grapes, Colonel Teixeira Mendes was fiercely rending his false Tower of Babel with blows of a military sword. Having previously cut several slices without effect, and after verifying the lack of any "Surprise!" therein, he savagely retaliated, wielding the alleged weapon, while his friends stole away in their underwear, to the interior of the house, and tried to summon the family doctor.

Sapristi!

The first scientist to study *Hevea brasiliensis*, the Frenchman Charles Marie de La Condamine, observing a game of ball among the Cambeba Indians, asserted that the rubber object was defying the laws of the earth's gravity.

The Pará Provincial

16 September, 1898

"*La Compagnie Opératique de la France*, directed by maestro François Blangis, is on its way!

"According to reports from several of the leading French papers, the *troupe* is composed of a number of first-rate *artistes*, including the *sensationnels* Justine L'Amour and Henri Munié, with whom any devotee of the lyrical drama is certainly familiar.

"It is assuredly to be expected that the upcoming lyrical season will have much to offer a public which has for too long been singularly deprived of so fortunate a diversion.

"The acting company includes: Madame Justine L'Amour, Munié himself, Matrat, Dubosca, Frédal, Boudier, Labégenski, Azancoth, Moreau, Marthe Alex, Concetta, Marie Annelli, Saverne, Zelmira Forloni, Michele Verse, Helene Andrée, Amelia Rossetti, and Linda Schiavi.

"Concert master and director of the orchestra: François Blangis Gémier.

"Set designer: Robert Boulingrin.

"Costumes: Mariana Taddio and Berthe Boulingrin.

"The *répertoire* of the company is richly diverse, and for the benefit of our readers we have published it below, in its entirety:

Verdi—AIDA, with ballet
Offenbach—LES CONTES D'HOFFMANN
Bizet—L'ARLESIENNE
Suppé—BOCCACCIO
Lecoq & Clairville—THE DAUGHTER OF
MADAME ANGOT
Chueca & Valverde—LA GRAN VIA (a zarzuela)
Offenbach—LA JOLIE PARFUMEUSE
Verney—D'ARTAGNAN

"A gala welcoming for the illustrious *troupe* is to be headed by the Mayor of Belém, along with a host of Paraensian notables. And of course, *Vive la France!*"

Science

Rubber has a rather equivocal consistency, and variations in temperature sorely affect its properties of malleableness and extensibility. In Belém, it is quite malleable. Once it reaches London, however, it has already become thoroughly intractable.

Biographical

I had been living in Belém since November of 1897, working as an editor for the *Pará Provincial*. My friend João Lúcio had given me the job, and put me in charge of international news. The paper enjoyed a prestigious reputation and its type had been imported from Germany. It operated out of a townhouse with large windows looking onto the Praça da República, the main square in Belém. In the heat of the abolitionist and republican struggles the journal had strengthened itself, and with the rubber boom it soon attracted the intelligentsia of a growing metropolis. It was one of the rare bulwarks of modernity in the troubled history of the provincial opposition press. And to belong to the opposition in Brazil is no slight task.

On the ground floor, with its doors protected by thick iron bars, was the front office. Then on the upper floor, the editorial operation itself with its heavy tables, tremendous inkwells, and beautiful collection of pens. To get there you had to climb up an English wrought-iron staircase, where the journalists had the habit of carrying on extended conversations before getting down to the business of the day. In the back of the editorial section, separated by a wooden partition, was the office of the editor-in-chief, João Lúcio. It presented a sober atmosphere, with two windows and a variety of Victorian furniture, bookcases housing bound law treatises and flanking a diligently disordered desk.

Expediency

I had finished translating two international items and was having a talk with João Lúcio, telling him about my situation with Cira, only to confess that it made me slightly uneasy. João Lúcio bantered about my fears and mentioned that he had been Cira's classmate, back in primary school. I told João Lúcio about the document concerning Acre, and he also became interested in it. I slapped him on the back, but left the office with the impression he was toying with me. João Lúcio had a friendly face, no doubt, but he hadn't convinced me with his ironic railleries that women are interested in secret documents only if they should happen to be private letters from lovers.

Adventurers Also Have Souls

At five in the evening, Cira would pass by the Café Abolition. By now I was certain she was not the best means for an adventurer to integrate himself into latex society. If that had been what I was after at the moment, I should obviously have rid myself of her presence. And to be honest, I was quite tired of my fugitive wanderings about the globe and had decided to establish myself in Belém, whatever the cost. Back in Buenos Aires, I had thought for a time of securing passage on a packet ship to India, to head for one of those countries that pertain more to fantasy than to geography. I might very well live in Macao, or Indonesia. I was nearly forty and still hadn't settled down in one place. I had lost my roots, but now I wanted to enrich myself and live in peace, anywhere, and eventually die in a comfortable study, with a black smoking jacket and some secret vice, well into my sixties. Then in March of '97, I was in Rio de Janeiro and working as a bookkeeper for the firm of Lourenço & Company, where I met up with Maldonado. A Biscayan from Bilbao, he had become a millionaire selling articles of toiletry in the Amazonas. It was he who convinced me to make the trip to Belém, with my more realistic project.

The Mysterious Gypsy

Today I realize that to be an adventurer one has to be totally bereft of discrimination. Precisely what I was, a man of no discrimination, who liked to experience the greatest possible contact with life around him. In my student days I visited a fair in Valladolid, where a gypsy prophesied that I would one day be acclaimed king. My classmates took pleasure in affirming that I had been born to put an end to the Bourbon dynasty and that King Alfonso XII had better beware. I had run across this gypsy in the autumn of '76, and since then, even the figure of the bourgeois gentleman I had in mind for myself developed his aristocratic touches. While I mechanically stamped passports in San Sebastián, I was already dreaming of becoming king of the white slaves, in Istanbul.

Parallel Action

The territory of Acre is situated on the globe at 9° south latitude and 70° west longitude. On this particular evening a group of latex gatherers were having a break from work on the property known as Bela Vista, belonging to Ubaldino Meireles. Colonel Ubaldino was in Manaus at the moment, on business, and the overseer had decided to allow a little evening get-together for the men. It would be a strange party, given that there were no women on the plantation (Colonel Ubaldino refused to hire married men at Bela Vista). The colonel's *seringueiros* would hold their festivity in the backyard of the "big house," and had been busily clearing the area of weeds since early morning. Two of them sitting on the back steps, with flute and guitar, were trying out a few tunes together. In front of the house a Brazilian flag unfurled in a momentary breeze, to the melody of a *chorinho*. By morning, however, the overseer would repent of his generosity and fail to satisfy Colonel Ubaldino with his explanation of the death of two *seringueiros*, slaughtered by machetes at the height of the drunkenness that was always the best part of the evening.

Ah, Love!

Once I was with Cira and her face close to mine, she could caress my neck with warm breath and sighs. Her arms encircling my shoulders as we kissed; her tongue a darting predator, as we fell into bed. Thus I began the ritual exploration of her body, until at a certain moment I discovered the most appealing pair of breasts my hands had ever encountered. I rolled one around in my palm like a cuddly little pet, while my mouth was delighting in the intermittent sallies of the above-named predator and the rest of my body took the initiative of blindly undressing her. I eagerly made my way through the delicate canyon of her small bosom, browned by the sun and warm with heat, the nipples turned apart like wary sentinels guarding their chest of treasure. Firm and full enough to inflame true cupidity. I began to greedily mine those feminine peaks throbbing to my lips, as the length of Cira in its apparent stillness stretched out far below. I could hardly resist going on to undress her, until finally discovering the dark hairs which forested the delicate plateau between her legs. When I commenced to also undress myself, scanning the evident terrain, my tree swung loose and swayed in the open air. Her limbs parted to receive me. . . .

Ghosts from the Past

Bereft of discrimination, an adventurer nonetheless has a past, just like anyone else. I was born on the morning of February 20th, 1859, in Cádiz, Spain. My parents were Fernando Luiz Galvez Concepción de Aria, Admiral of the Royal Navy, and Rosaura Rodrigues de Aria, whose talents were domestic. Queen Isabella II ruled Spain, while married to her impotent cousin Francisco Assis de Bourbon. My father died in 1896, and my mother two months later, of profound melancholy. That was when I discovered that my father had been an enthusiastic gambler and hadn't left me an inheritance. In fact, he hadn't left me anything.

In 1868, my father had participated in the rebellion at Cádiz, and I got to see the troops exchanging gunfire along the Isthmus of San Fernando. The military wanted to have done with the "spurious race of Bourbons." My father would live to run the gamut of political possibility in Spain, from Commander of the Fleet to imprisonment once the monarchy was restored, in 1875. Perhaps for that very reason, my father had a sense of humor as unpredictable as the sea. When he fell into disgrace, my mother fled with me to Ceuta, where we would remain for the next year. She was a decisive woman: her own father, a relic of the guerrilla war against the troops of Napoleon Bonaparte, had died of bubonic plague somewhere in the Sahara, leaving my mother in the most abject state of misery.

We lived on the Alameda de Cádiz, in a small but stately mansion with a mirador that overlooked the sea. It was an old, Moorish dwelling and its mirador afforded a splendid view of the Bay of Cádiz—and to the right, off in the distance, the violet thread of the San Petri River. It was on this terrace that we would always assemble as a family, and I would listen to mother tell fantastic adventure stories about Spanish soldiers and sweating Berbers, armed with scimitars. Mother embroidered with precise gestures, her fingernails or the golden ring she wore adroitly aligning a thread delineating a scene of Spanish galleons and pirate treasure. A dark-skinned Penelope. . . .

Nocturnal Conspiring

Thursday, September 20. I took a coach out to the old Estrada do Val-de-Cães. I got out in front of an abandoned mill and observed light coming from a garret window. I climbed the stairs and groped along in the dark until, out of breath, I reached a large attic with a low ceiling, where I found myself surrounded by abandoned machines, each looking like a remarkable piece of rusty sculpture. A choice locale for a clandestine rendezvous in a cloak-and-dagger novel. Precisely why I was there, of course. . . . Face to face with none other than João Lúcio and Cira, in the company of three others. A student of law who was drumming his fingers and coughing occasionally. A satirical poet with the face of a satirical poet. And a lawyer with a Britannic air about him, but with the face of an Indian who had little to do with poetry, satirical or otherwise. Therein assembled was the Committee for the Defense of Acre.

Political Picture

The state of Amazonas was at odds with the state of Pará. The government of Amazonas was discreetly supporting Acre as a Brazilian cause. The government of Pará, on the other hand, had adopted the federal position of considering Acre a Bolivian territory.

The three gentlemen mentioned above had tried to seize Trucco, when I prevented them—remember? Cira and João Lúcio were after my help. But I was in no position to recruit even mosquitoes to defend Acre.

My Politics

I didn't like the Americans—that was the only sentiment I could muster at the moment. I knew that the Americans, in the name of humanity, were busy taking advantage of Spain's desperation in Cuba and elsewhere. I knew also that the Spanish army was acting in a brutal manner. There were concentration camps, torture, and assassinations. Many a Cuban nationalist had already died by the hand of Spanish executioners. The Americans, hungering for Cuban sugar, had arrived with their troop of roughnecks and had butchered the Spanish soldiers retreating along the coast of San Tiago de Cuba. A similar action was occurring in the Philippines. The Americans apparently considered themselves a new knight-errantry and had money. I would do everything I could to outflank them.

The Revolutionary

Picture me with my flints and my Brown Bessie, a skinny figure with English colonial hat, wandering through a jungle brimming with naked savages: Dr. Galvez Livingstone, I presume!

Eros and Revolution

Cira by no means attempted to induce me to fight for love's sake. Confronting American imperialism with love for a woman as the ideological impetus? I would simply say, please, my dear, this isn't a novel by the Abbé Prévost! How many pounds sterling are we talking about?

Minutes of the Meeting

Committee for the Defense of Acre,
Gathered in the Year of Our Lord Jesus Christ One Thousand Eight Hundred and Ninety-eight, at 10:10 p.m., in a location known as the Old Mill, on the Estrada do Val-de-Cães. The meeting was called to order by our president, João Lúcio de Azevedo, who introduced the special guest of the evening, a Mr. Luiz Galvez Rodrigues de Aria. The first speaker to ask for the floor was our comrade-in-arms Cira Chermont: "The cause we defend invokes no exception to nationality. It simply invokes solidarity. Together, we struggle to ward off the threat that hangs over Acre and its people—a wretched, forgotten land which has unexpectedly become the target of intense international greed."

Comrade-in-arms Alberto Leite offered an aside: "Specifically, we are struggling to prevent the formation of any international corporation with the aim of dominating Acre. So many regions around the globe have already come to lament the presence of such enterprises. Zanzibar is a prime example."

Comrade-in-arms Cira Chermont at this point resumed: "Our finest rubber comes from Acre. For the first half of this century no one even debated the nationality of Acre. Only Indians lived there, and Acre was avoided by even the most audacious explorers. After all, there was nothing but fever there. The Cearensians had no fear of fever, however, and they settled the region. Pushing back the frontier with their own misery . . ."

Maxim

Of course, misery is also imperialistic.

Minutes (continued)

". . . and the one who benefited was Brazil. Today, the rubber from Acre commands an excellent price on the market, so Bolivia—at the instigation of English and American bankers—is demanding the territory for herself. And Minister Aramayo, with his copper mines in Tupiza, wishes to hand Acre over to an international corporation of some kind. We still don't have the positive proof of this, but should it turn out to be so, it would be a dangerous precedent for South America, even catastrophic."

President João Lúcio thereupon interjected: "The worst is that President Campos Sales is entangling Brazil in a treaty of boundaries that flies in the face of reality. Intimidated by international pressures, fearful of the loss of credits, he seems bent upon yielding up Acre to the capitalists."

Comrade-in-arms Cira Chermont once again proceeded: "There is presently a document in the hands of the Consul General from Bolivia. Mr. Galvez witnessed when the American consul handed it over. I was also in Luiz Trucco's presence when the transaction took place, at the latter's home. I am certain of the document's importance and of its relation to the international corporation in question."

At this point, Mr. Luiz Galvez himself took the floor: "It is true that I was present when Mr. Michael Kennedy delivered an envelope to the Consul General from Bolivia, the contents of which appear to have dealt with Acre— Luiz Trucco proclaimed as much himself. Yet I don't see in what manner I can be of help."

Cira Chermont thereupon interjected: "We wish you to obtain the said document."

Mr. Luiz Galvez immediately took exception: "But that

would be theft! And I happen to be a foreigner, subject to the laws of extradition."

Cira Chermont again spoke up: "Theft? Nonsense, a simple case of documentation, for which we would guarantee your protection."

President João Lúcio then took the floor: "With such a document, Mr. Galvez, we would possess a powerful weapon of denunciation."

Mr. Luiz Galvez once again came to the floor: "Ladies and gentlemen, for the time being I shall place friendship above the caprice of politics. And therefore I accept the task you lay before me. . . . I wish to make it clear, however, that I feel at liberty to disassociate myself from any further obligation in the matter."

President João Lúcio heartily interjected: "Our movement, in any case, will know how to show its appreciation in future."

Mr. Luiz Galvez thereupon concluded: "I will need a week to obtain the document."

President João Lúcio at this point resumed the floor: "Granted. We shall hold our next meeting on the 26th."

The present meeting was thus adjourned, these minutes having been recorded by the undersigned First Secretary Lemos Nogueira Filho and thereupon read and approved by those present, whose signatures are likewise affixed hereunder.

Femme Fatale

Cira, treacherous one! You back me against a wall, provoking me to accede to an imponderable undertaking. . . . I pressed the woman to my chest, the better to feel the two hemispheres of flesh. Cira accused me of being hardly realistic, so I asked her what it meant to be realistic.

Reality of the Adventure

You came in search of riches, my angel (she was accustomed to calling me that), and around here you only make money in latex. Somehow I can't quite picture you with a machete, chopping away at the trunk of a rubber tree. Or running yourself into debt at the central trading post, a classic case of Amazonian sociology. . . .

Sociology I

She hit the mark, all right, and I realized that I needed all the friends I had in order not to have to take the latex trail.

Sociology II

The latex trail in the Amazon is not part of the same system that links Paris and Amsterdam.

Of Love and Latex

The moon began to nudge the horizon between slender silhouettes of cabbage palm. The two of us were stretched out on the grass, in back of Cira's house. Her husband was upstairs sleeping, and I was busy intending to rob a document. The darkened windows of an immense house and the texture of Cira's long hair, spread upon the lawn. It was difficult to escape the destiny of an adventurer.

My Thoughts

I had been given a week to obtain the document but was in no mood to go near Trucco's home. I would run into João Lúcio, over at the paper, and act evasively. Drawing upon my stock of laconic gestures, I would purse my lips together and widen my eyes, which could be interpreted equally as meaning that everything was fine or that I was having a problem. My mania for being ambiguous. . . . And I no longer put in appearances at the Café Abolition. I would leave the office and go buy a bottle of Cognac. Then go up to my room in the Hotel Riachuelo and drink until early morning.

THE EMPEROR OF THE AMAZON

A Good Memory

On those nights of Cognac and chastity I would re-member the lines from Cervantes' *Galatea*: *"If to the weary traveler/ it unexpectedly befall,/ that by some surreptitious design/ he be forced to flee before/ the long awaited shel-ter,/ for which with so vain a haste/ he had restlessly strived,/ would he not clearly be/ confused by the dark fears,/ whch night and the stillness/ offer all around? /And even more so,/ if rosy dawn herself/ —O let her wings not fail me!—/ deign too late to offer/ her serene and precious light? /Then am I he that travels/ to reach this fortunate abode,/ and though close I seem/ to that fugitive shadow,/ once called repose,/ I fear I do mistake,/ for the good that flees,/ the grief that abounds."*

Social History

The rubber forests of Amazonia were termed "native" and produced rubber of varied quality. Some rubber gath-erers, after better prices, would mix impurities into the product to increase its weight. Rubber was sold by the kilo and this practice became widespread. At a given moment in social history, the rubber buyers came to con-fuse the word "native" with "impure." And English and American buyers, preoccupied with the purity of the product, dreamed of controlling its "native" sources.

Youth

Since I have a week to obtain the document and wish to avoid the problem, I beg the reader's forbearance while I digress a little about my youth. In 1879, I entered the University of Seville, where I pursued a program of study in Juridical and Social Sciences. Spain was seething with agitation, and Seville was a bastion of conservatism. In fact, Seville had always defended the monarchy. The university itself, however, was a center of heated debate. Anarchists and conservatives alike mingled with the students.

I was altogether aloof from politics, considering myself an *aficionado* in bohemian terrorism. I would wander with my guitarist friends from café to café throughout the Alcazar, and I can tell you I wasn't impressed by anyone or anything. A regular enough student, I suppose, I learned to speak French, English, and Portuguese. I enjoyed my carousing and never chose to forego any women out of twinges of conscience. In the summers, I preferred a more intimate setting. I would install myself up in my room at the *pensión* over in the Barrio de Santa Cruz, with a bottle of wine and a mistress. As you can see, I spent my youth in the traditional manner: women, fiestas, flamenco dancing, and my studies—in exactly that order.

By the time I finished my studies, I was the fiancé of Paula Mercedes Mudejar. Ah, Paula! . . . so pure and sweet it was nauseating. She was heiress to the fortune of Don Fernando Rivadavia y Churroguera Mudejar, wine-grower and cigarette manufacturer. Through the good graces of Don Fernando, I managed to obtain a post in the diplomatic corps. I went to work in San Sebastián, at the summer palace of the king. I should have married Paula in 1886, but was saved by the death of King Alfonso XII, which postponed our scheduled wedding until the summer of '87. Obviously, the marriage was not meant to be, and my courtship would end in rather a tempestuous fashion, like everything I seem to do in life.

Theft

Midnight. I enter the house of Luiz Trucco with a blue neckerchief tied around my face. The butler is awakened and I threaten him with a pistol. Trucco comes in in his bathrobe, to see what's going on, his face still pasty with sleep. With an American accent, I demand the document. He offers no resistance, handing me a blue envelope. I examine it quickly, confirming its contents, then take to my heels while letting out a bloodcurdling laugh.

Correction!

Excuse me, but at this point I find myself obliged—out of respect for the truth—to interrupt our hero, something I will do whenever he fails to relate the facts of the matter. He did, in fact, manage to obtain the document, but in the most prosaic manner possible. On the day in question Luiz Galvez was at a restaurant on Largo da Pólvora, enjoying a fried chicken. The restaurant was nearly empty and a few sleepy-eyed *cocottes* were chatting with the idle waiters. Luiz Galvez eventually walked out, irritated with the service at the restaurant. He caught a hackney coach and headed for Trucco's house, where he took the liberty of collapsing into a comfortable chair, there in the consul's study. It was unbearably hot, that day, with black clouds weighing heavily in the skies of Belém. Trucco was fanning himself with a sheet of paper, wiping his face with a handkerchief and staring out the window. The two of them at that point would have given a week's salary for one breath of air. Trucco finally picked up the morning paper and began to read, his forehead still dripping. The light was poor; a heavy shower began to fall. Trucco asked Luiz Galvez if he wouldn't mind translating the document for him, since there was no one else he could trust with such a matter. At the moment, however, the document was not in Trucco's possession, so he made a date with Luiz Galvez, to hand over the same to him, at another reception to be given in the house of Dona Irene. Trucco also offered a post in his consulate to Luiz Galvez, telling him it was dangerous to work for the *Pará Provincial*.

Civilization

A newspaper in Rio de Janeiro informed its readers that the Amazon was nothing but a highly touted Hottentotia.

Political Relativity

A conservative in Paris could well be a revolutionary in Belém. In an immature land, even the Gospel is inflammatory.

Márcio Souza

Out on the Street

I was walking down the street toward the Café Abolition
when I noticed that the confectionary shop of Domenico
Lizzano was closed. I was nevertheless unmoved by the
tragedy: Lizzano was in the clink. I walked in on the buzz
of conversation at the café, and the waiter came by with
tray in hand. I ordered the usual, a glass of *jerez*, and
found myself a seat. Suddenly, Cira was tugging the arm
of my coat and dragged me outside in full view of everyone. Indiscreet, or exhibitionist?

From One Alcove . . .

Stretched out on one side of the bed, I was smoking a
cigarette and staring at a reproduction of *The Death of
Ophelia*, by Delacroix. Cira had brought me to this alcove
herself, and I must say I liked her audaciousness. We
struggled in the white sheets.

Contraband

Sir Henry Wickham stole seventy thousand rubber seeds
from the state of Amazonas. He told the customs officer
that they were intended for the queen's orchidarium. A
Victorian white lie, which worked. . .

Mischief II

Another party at the home of the mayor. Dona Irene
wished to redeem herself. Dona Eudóxia played another
waltz with those same sausage fingers, and some local poet
indulged in mythological mischief with a host of Olym-
pian deities. Sky without clouds, and punch. The mayor
away on a trip. In the street, the hustle and bustle of
traffic; while inside, the governor was quietly discussing
certain anonymous letters. Eventually Dona Irene recited
from the epics of Tasso, as proof of her culture. Trucco
began to amuse the governor with the image of odalisques
in Acre. To my way of thinking, any Acrean odalisques

would quickly die of gonorrhea, so I decided to steal away from such tedious conversation. Dona Irene took me by the arm, to show me her collection of rare cheeses.

Rochefort

Greasy shelves of sweaty discs, cubes, and wedges. Dona Irene was licking the salt from her fingers, sitting on a wicker sofa, proffering an exotic specimen from Tunisia. Parmesan? I asked in utter ignorance. Dona Irene was so amused by her own superiority that—impulsively—she lunged toward me. I let my hands flutter through the air and around her voluminous body until I finally encompassed a vast waist. She invited me to move on to more intimate surroundings. We walked to the bedroom, munching a soft Camembert, like two naughty children.

. . . To Another

I sat on the austere bed of His Honor the Mayor. White mosquito netting hung from the ceiling, tied back with ribbons. Dona Irene began to unbutton my clothes (I had clearly assumed the passive role), then stopped to let her dress fall and free her body from its massive corset. I confess I felt somewhat intimidated, being practically flung upon the bed while she kneaded my body with her fingers. My Valencian provolone, she whispered to me. There was a knock on the door and I leaped for the closet —a classic maneuver, given that what we heard was the voice of the mayor, calling for his wife as he dropped his suitcases to the floor. Dona Irene, however, preferred to stuff me under the bedstead, and then went over to open the door. She was clutching a hand to her heart, and confessed to her husband a slight indisposition. I saw two legs barge in, and almost died of laughter when His Honor's tweed pants fell to the floor. The bed shook with violence above my head. Taking advantage of the conjugal enthusiasm, I began to crawl across the floor, making my way toward the half-open door of the bedroom. I got up and slipped out, just as the couple reached their climax. I sighed at the same instant, in homage to them. In the living room, Dona Eudóxia was playing the piano by herself, and I began to feel slightly nauseous from the taste of cheese in my mouth.

Aside

It was at this party that Luiz Trucco actually delivered the document to our hero, for translation. The incident with Dona Irene may well be authentic.

San Sebastián

I couldn't sleep that night. My life could never make a serious story, only a theme for a *feuilleton*. And life in Belém never passed for more than the cynical banter of a soap opera. I was frightened one day I might be tortured with cheeses. I could hear the bells of the cathedral, bells that took me back to 1887, in San Sebastián, where I was trying to bag the virginal breasts of Paula Mudejar. The court was transferred back to the city, and there I met the Duchess Theresse Von Zienssine, married to a Spanish nobleman and in possession of vast holdings on the Lower Rhine. Theresse was a genuine product of German well-being who loved lavish suppers, flamenco dancing, and voracious sex. None of which her syphilitic husband could share with her. We met one another at a restaurant, but ended the evening in the alcove of her palazzo. Our meetings became so evident that, among the tables and bedrooms of San Sebastián, no one spoke of anything else. Her husband heard it from a sacristan and was not pleased by the news. Paula Mudejar also found out and broke off our engagement, after attempting suicide by drinking three liters of wine. I was transferred to Rome. I had lost Don Fernando's little opera cigar case.

Behind Closed Doors

The little windows of the attic were open, but the heat was still suffocating. Reunited was the Committee for the Defense of Acre.

The Clarity of a Document

STATE DEPARTMENT. Foreign Office.

THE UNITED STATES OF AMERICA, through diplomatic means with the Republic of Brazil, will gestate the recognition of the rights of the Republic of Bolivia to the territories of Acre, Purus, and Iaco, presently occupied in accordance with rights established by the Treaty of 1867.

THE UNITED STATES OF AMERICA pledges to make available to the Republic of Bolivia whatever amount of military specie the latter may need in the event of a war with the Republic of Brazil.

THE UNITED STATES OF AMERICA shall insist upon the Republic of Brazil's naming, within the current year, a Commission, which, in accord with the Republic of Bolivia, may fix the definitive frontiers between Purus and Javari.

THE REPUBLIC OF BRAZIL shall have to grant navigation rights along the tributaries of the Rio Amazonas to barks of Bolivian registry, as well as allow free passage through customs, in Pará and in Manaus, to merchandise destined for Bolivian ports.

THE REPUBLIC OF BOLIVIA shall grant to the United States of America, as recompense for their good offices, a 50% reduction in customs duties on rubber being shipped to any port of the said nation, and this abatement shall remain in effect for a period lasting ten years.

THE REPUBLIC OF BOLIVIA, in the event of having to declare war against the Republic of Brazil, will renounce the Treaty of 1867, will agree to a border line running from Bolivia to Boca do Acre, and will deliver the remaining territory—which is to say, the zone encompassed between Boca do Acre and the actual limits of occupation —to the United States of America, in free and absolute title and possession.

WASHINGTON, 9th of May, 1898.

Mission Accomplished

I received a sincere thanks from everyone and learned that life is much like a drama in which present and future commingle in a logic of abandonment. In Paris, I once had an anarchist friend who was blown through the air while attempting an assassination. He had left in my care a packet of pamphlets wrapped in yellow paper. When I learned of the manner in which he had died—no head, a mangled trunk—I felt a mixture of shock and repugnance, indicating to me once and for all my inaptitude for the comedy of bureaucracy. Veiled anarchists hardly make good diplomats.

Sun Plus Art

In the midst of applause, Justine L'Amour waved with a fan while descending the gangway. Two sailors deferentially assisted the *chanteuse* beneath a shower of flowers. From the bridge of the S.S. *Raethia*, the captain saluted the waiting multitude. Justine appeared to be exhausted and irked by the heat. Blangis walked down the gangplank behind the prima donna, with the air of a Roman senator.

An Incident

Blangis, trying to brace himself as he slipped on the stairway, tore off a lace shawl from a lady who was also disembarking. An intellectual on shore began to read aloud from his academic address, while the mayor busied himself delivering gallantries to the prima donna. Blangis, by now, was wearing the shawl; and stevedores began lowering the baggage, graciously exempted from customs. The *artistes* for the upcoming operatic season were, after all, official guests of the state of Pará.

THE EMPEROR OF THE AMAZON

An Impression

Justine L'Amour confessed to the mayor that the Rio Amazonas could hardly be compared to the Garonne. And she constantly resorted to the expression *la-bas*, for Brazil.

Quai d'Hospice

The passenger from whom Blangis had lifted the shawl was English, and at the moment waving a pound note in front of the nose of an offended customs officer. Noticing that our Frenchman had transformed her shawl into a scarf, she gathered her courage and attempted to retrieve the item from him. The two began tugging at either end, until Blangis suddenly let go. The woman went flying across the dock and landed among several bunches of ripe bananas, where she sat tearfully rueing her trip to South America.

Mission in the Tropics

Blangis and Justine L'Amour had brought with them civilization. The passenger seated upon the bananas, however, was here on an evangelical mission, a colonel in the Salvation Army. The colonel had left behind her tranquil Southwood, upon learning to her horror (from an issue of *Tropical Life*) that, in the Amazon jungle, poor natives were enslaved by the rich ones, who only wished to bask in the laps of liquor and lust. Seated upon the bruised bunches of that typically tropical fruit, she began to have doubts about her mission of temperance and morality. The natives, aside from being debauched and alcoholic, were obviously *loco*, a state with respect to which the evangelist felt at a decided disadvantage.

Déjeuné sur l'Herbe

I was enjoying a custard under the protection of an arbor of creepers, out in the back garden of Cira's home.

I had lunched with the Chermont couple, and Alberto told me of his plans to go to the waters of Vichy. Then Cira invited me for a stay at their plantation on the Isle of Marajó. Alberto agreed I should, and offered us the use of a launch from his lumber company. The day was marvelous and perfumed, with that tentative spring weather the climate of Pará is apt to occasionally bestow.

Promenade

Cira planned to escape the Candlelight-Nazareth festivities, a religious celebration given over to popular enjoyment and tradition. I'd never had the opportunity to be present at a Nazareth festival, but it was obviously something important to the daily life of Pará, given that the opera season was set by the event.

Work

I was translating a news item concerning the Dreyfus case, while João Lúcio told me of his interview with Justine L'Amour and Blangis. The magnesium of the photographer had unfortunately failed to ignite, so there were no photographs. The prima donna had spoken of gales upon the high seas, as well as sundry Gallic matters. Blangis had explained to him that the company was en route from the Caribbean. Actually, as far as João Lúcio was concerned, this was just another of those companies, without any future, that venture *aux pays latins* from time to time. I mentioned to him that I wouldn't be back until the following week, that I was going to Marajó Island with Cira. He nodded his head knowingly.

Telegram

divulge document stop vaez

Moment of Doubt

João Lúcio read the telegram which had arrived from Manaus, then remembered the expectant eyes of Justine L'Amour.

THE EMPEROR OF THE AMAZON

The Isle of Marajó

I wouldn't have known it was an island if we weren't looking at a map. The plantation was very impressive. All the while, back in Belém, my destiny was unfolding. Yet we were quite contented to eat trifles and drink wine. And in the background, cotton fields as far as the eye could see, to the natural limits of the jungle. We fished from a canoe, but never caught any fish.

Democracy

When the governor arrived, Trucco practically attacked him in his study, brandishing a crumpled newspaper. Paes de Carvalho thought that a new revolution must have erupted in Acre.

Democratic Dialogue

TRUCCO: Excellency, have you read the *Provincial*?
PAES DE CARVALHO: No, I haven't had time yet. Why?
TRUCCO: I'm victim of a nefarious betrayal!
PAES DE CARVALHO: Nefarious betrayal? By whom?
TRUCCO: Read the paper!
PAES DE CARVALHO: Sons of bitches! How could they say a thing like that? Me, a patriot, allied with the Americans? This is terrible, terrible! Sons of bitches....
TRUCCO: A complete scandal, I'm ruined!
PAES DE CARVALHO: It was better when we had Floriano; the press at least knew its place then.
TRUCCO: Somebody paid them to do this. . . .
PAES DE CARVALHO: My government will fall.
TRUCCO: Your excellency must take forceful measures.
PAES DE CARVALHO: As for that, you needn't worry —Lieutenant Fonseca! Bring me the chief of police, immediately!

Romanza

Cira caught a butterfly and started examining the insect with a magnifying glass. It was raining that night. The roof tiles hissed with wetness, and there was an odor of damp earth in the air. Come morning, the sun broke through the clouds and Cira woke me. I had slept in an armchair. The moon clung to the sky on that luxuriant morning, and we went for a swim in the cool water. Cira dove in first.

Morning Edition

João Lúcio was unenthusiastically preparing the next edition of the paper. He knew that he had poked a hornets' nest with a very short stick. The *Pará Provincial* had gone on the stands, and by nine o'clock there were no more copies to be found. Yet it would seem to have been an ephemeral triumph, to use João Lúcio's expression. Various well-known political elements were to be seen prowling around outside, and João Lúcio kept pacing back and forth in his office. By midday, police had surrounded the building.

Philosophy of an Adventurer

Cira claimed that, in Pará, romanticism wasn't consumptive, it was epileptic. She also told me that I was the last truly romantic adventurer in the Amazon. Could it be that I really had no other talent? Evidently I could at least recognize my own limitations. I smiled at her the way an opportunistic adventurer was supposed to. You see, in those days it took a certain refinement to be an opportunist. Adventurism was not pejorative in the political sense.

Democracy in the Provinces

Five local flics strode into the office of the paper and brusquely invaded João Lúcio's private partition, overturning everything while ordering the journalist to stand aside with his hands on his head. João Lúcio tried to resist and they slammed him. They hurled the gross volumes of law at his head, and he began to bleed from the lips. They were also hoping to find a certain Spaniard, but contented themselves for the moment with shoving João

Lúcio out into the street. The bust of Voltaire looked on impassively. In the pressroom, meantime, some ten men armed with iron pipes proceeded to smash the presses. A crowd of the curious saw when João Lúcio came out, his shirt covered with blood. João Lúcio saw the crowd as well, and heard the noise of iron pipes destroying the presses, a cacophony of sounds quite common to national politics. João Lúcio began to sing the *Marseillaise*.

Return

A light drizzle was falling when we left Marajó Island. The launch broke the leather belting of the rudder on a muddy shallow, and we were stuck for a good three hours. The rain had stopped and we suffered an attack of tiny *pium* mosquitoes. I had ceased to extol Amazonian ecology. . . .

Plus and Minus

We reached the shores of Belém by late afternoon. We had tickets for the premiere of the opera season. The Nazareth festivities were over, leaving a balance of eight violent ends—folkloric excesses.

A Scintillating Evening

I stood staring concentratedly into the mirror at a knot my fingers were attempting to adjust in my minuscule green tie. Trotting horses were pulling carriages along the promenade of the Praça da República. Everyone stepped down, tipping hats and nodding heads, stroking beards, showing teeth, and milling around the ticket booth, moving up to the wrought-iron grating that protected the ticket vendor. Horses snorted with dilating nostrils and gentlemen stretched their starched collars with a finger—rapidly, so no one would notice. And with each passing moment more and more people congregated, because the opera was hardly something to be taken lightly. From inside the

Teatro da Paz, the sound of the orchestra tuning up: bows gliding over strings of the violoncellos; bassoons punctuating the heads which turned to and fro, offering one another a variety of intelligent glances. Ladies sparkling in their diamond brooches, palpitation of breasts and pearls. I finally conquered the knot of my tie and donned my top hat, checking out the polished tips of my black pair of shoes, where I caught my own distorted reflection, an indication of the shine.

The Opera

Cira and Alberto had gone on ahead of me, and met Dona Irene wearing a blue dress with embroidered nymphs and fauns in amorous pursuit. The couple were already ascending the staircase, in the direction of their box, when Cira noticed that Walter was making frantic signs, near one of the windows. At that point she learned what had happened to João Lúcio. She also found out that I was to be arrested.

Commemorazzione Verdiana

Rustle of silks, iambic-pentameter stares, and in the semidarkness the melancholy chords of the opening. Suffocating heat and perfume. It was a sad opera, to be sure, of the vintage variety. Even the dragging of chairs by latecomers, mixed with smiles of pardon, failed to diminish the poignant mood of those violins. And once again the age-old hostilities of an ancient civilization would compact perdition for the dark-skinned Nubian slave, named Aida, and her lover, Radamès. Cira, my aristocratic mistress, was nervously eyeing the paltry sets; the restless spectators were more richly attired than the players themselves.

Giuseppe, Still

Cira, in a mannerly fashion, straightened the folds of her lavish gown. With thumb and forefinger she lifted opera glasses to her lovely eyes, scanning the auditorium, searching for her straggling adventurer.

> "*Celeste Aida, forma divina,*
> *mistico serto di luce e fior,*
> *del mio pensiero tu sei regina,*
> *tu di mia vita sei lo splendor.*"

Her petulant mouth must be tremulous by now, imaging me already in the clutches of the police and undergoing a brutal interrogation: fetid breath and spittle; the stinging lash of a manatee switch, lacerating my palms.

A long aria floated up from the stage, drifting through her thoughts, sung by a Gallic Aida who was at the moment clutching the waist of her shabbily dressed—but haughtily demeanored—Radamès!

> RADAMÈS: "*Nume, che duce ed arbitro*
> *sei d'ogni umana guèrra,*
> *protegi tu, difendi*
> *d'Egitto il sacro suol.*"

Opera Glasses I

Discreet and melodious brass, for an enchanting ballet by the female slaves of Amneris. A casual whisper, though, immediately drew the opera glasses away from the stage. Colonel Tristão was exploring the powdered flesh of Léia Frasão, a maiden predisposed to the pomp of life, probably from teaching Brazilian history at the local lycée. (Cira didn't even seem to notice—where could Galvez be?—the middle finger of the colonel's left hand making taut the dark nipple of Léia's right breast.) Austere, perhaps, but without a rigid set of rules to govern her conduct outside the classroom, Léia froze at the tip of the colonel's long, longing, longest finger. Cira, meanwhile, had turned away toward another box . . . and another . . . end of the first act. I arrived, eventually, quite late to the theater. The Moors were already dancing with their long-plumed fans.

Entr'acte

Dona Irene, who lacked all good sense, was also looking for me. The second act was underway, when her heart suddenly leapt between the la- and ti-notes of the trumpets. The Grand March.

Opera Glasses II

Trumpets, chorus, winds, orchestra, ballet, nothing troubled Governor Paes de Carvalho any longer: so exhausted was he, by provocation and intrigue, he was sound asleep on the velvet cushions of his curtained loge.

Beside him, quite awake for the moment, was the mayor —provoked and intrigued, however. Dona Irene had left during intermission (to look for me) and was taking a long time to return.

End of the second act, so as not to exhaust the reader's patience.

Moon Above the Nile

> *"Qui Radamès verrà . . . che vorrà dirmi?*
> *Io tremo . . . Ah! se tu vieni*
> *a recarmi, o crudel, l'ultimo addio,*
> *del Nilo i cupi vortici*
> *mi daranno tomba . . ."*

A box in the second balcony, where I was seated between two young ladies, friends of mine and fine specimens who were entertaining themselves by picking out young men in the audience down below. Meanwhile, Aida was lamenting.

Oh God! That cardboard coconut palm is about to fall any second—saved, thank heavens, by a timely curtain down on act three. Applause. . . . I went to the men's lounge to smoke a cigarette.

Temple of Vulcan

The priests intone their hymns of wrath. Cira watched while Dona Irene entered my box and put her hands over my eyes. Darkness, skin (rough to the touch). I smile and my lady friends smile also. Lugubrious brass *andante*. . . .

Opera Glasses III

Dona Irene was whispering something to me in a rather suspect manner. I needed to flee, she told me, and my legs buckled (a hero isn't made of iron). She repeated the message in more caressing tones, but this time provided the motives. I jumped up and tried to leave. Cira observed me, holding her breath. Dona Irene suddenly dragged me into the ladies' room and turned the lock. She kissed me wetly, her mouth like an overripe cheese, while pinching my shoulders and lifting her long dress.

The Crypt

> *"Vedi? . . . Di morte l'angelo*
> *radiante a noi s'apressa . . .*
> *Degli anni tuoi nel fiore*
> *fuggir la vita!"*

The ladies' room smelled of urine. I made a decision: I slapped Dona Irene. I was frantic, and so I repeated the dose several times more. Dona Irene was speechless, pale, incredulous. She fell, nearly faint with fear, and let out a hoarse scream. I unlocked the door and flung myself headlong into the corridor. Dona Irene, however, refused to desist and came crawling out on all fours, howling like a madwoman in a gothic romance.

Duetto Finale

RADAMÈS: *"Il tripudio dei Sacerdoti . . .*
AIDA: *Il nostro inno di morte . . ."*

I was thunderstruck by the agility of that woman, even
on all fours and soaked with urine. My amazement lost
me a few seconds. She screamed, on her knees now, and
I ran toward the stairway. From the orchestra pit the
brasses were echoing Aida's theme, while the timpani
punctuated the rhythm, with contrabass. People were
stepping out of their boxes to see what was going on, and
a group of policemen were scurrying up the stairs. I
quickly stepped back, which they saw as suspicious.

Duetto Buffo

DONA IRENE: He attacked me! He tried to rape me, a
married woman!
RADAMÈS: *"O terra, addio, addio, valle de pianti!*
Sogno de gaudio che in dolor svanì!"

I ran back into the box where my two young ladies
were; they looked terrified, but ignorant of what was taking
place. I heard the mayor shout something, and my poor
friends began to cry. Radamès, meanwhile, was attempting
vainly to lift the cardboard slab.

DONA IRENE: It's him! The Spanish anarchist . . .
AIDA & RADAMÈS: *"A noi si schiude il ciel, e l'alme*
erranti volano al raggio dell'eterno
dì."

Variazione Verdiana

A police officer took out his whistle and sounded the
alarm. I jumped from the box into the auditorium below,

and many of the spectators also began to run. I heard the murmur of stunned voices as my body plummeted through space and fell to the carpet. I got up and saw myself surrounded by police. I attacked, distributing punches. I saw a tooth fly through the air in the direction of a chandelier. I climbed up onto the stage, and pandemonium broke loose. Many gentlemen, without knowing for sure what it was that was happening, parried policemen who were running through the auditorium like madmen, shoving ladies aside and leaving a trail of perspiration connoting abysmal hygienic habits. Several shots rang out.

Aida was stretched out in the crypt still, while Radamès stared incredulously, first at me and then at the maelstrom of civil guards scrambling up onto the stage. I passed by him like a bolt of lightning and sought refuge (befittingly!) in the Temple of Vulcan. The police had begun to scale the lofty walls of Egyptian profiles and hieroglyphics. The royal priests were struck dumb. Justine L'Amour, the *diva massima*, finally lifted her head and, observing the turmoil, let out a lovely piercing scream and fainted into the arms of Henri Munié (the former Radamès).

The orchestra had ceased, among squeaks and crushed instruments—a pharaonic confusion, if the reader will permit the phrase. The police, however, didn't seem the least interested in my person, exchanging punches with gentlemen in the audience, wrestling with the performers on stage, and waging a generally quixotic campaign on several fronts at once. I finally reached the wings, and without even a parting farewell to the chorus girls busy crying backstage, I made good my escape—through a back exit, naturally; as befits a *feuilleton*.

Triumph

Intrepid Paraensian Police, unparalleled in all of South America: defeating the armed might of a pharaoh.

Curtain Call

Mango and fig trees along the Praça da República. Cira was waiting for me in her carriage. A demonstration of bravado. . . . She spirited us to the harbor and handed me a bank draft. We vacillated, Cira insisting and myself refusing. I didn't want to accept such an offer, knowing how difficult it would be to ever see Cira again. I could never pay off that debt. She simply folded the draft and slipped it into my pocket, a command. I obeyed, then said goodbye and thanks in a soft voice. Nor was she deceived. . . .

Voyage

The dockside lull of early-morning hours. A steamer about to cast off from the quay. I sprang aboard and hid myself. Afterward, I would plan my future destiny. Crankings, whistles, rocking, and clanging. Cira vanished into darkness and the steamer put off at half speed. At least it was heading upriver.

PART TWO

*Up the vast,
dark
Rio Amazonas*

Tell me, dare I to accept/what happened in my fantasy/ while I slept?/Am I where I seem to be?/Yet why conjecture,/no one challenges me, here.

—Calderón, LIFE IS A DREAM

Cabotage

In this second part of the story our hero, making his
way up the Rio Amazonas, travels the nearly nine hundred
miles that separate Belém from Manaus. There exist in
this region 218 species of mosquitoes already classified
by scientists.

Awakening

I hadn't even noticed that the hold smelled of rosewood
and incense. I had stolen aboard the steamer in darkness,
and only now, with daylight pouring into the hold, could
I make out its general contours, which immediately brought
to mind the image of a floating dungeon. Through a dam-
aged top hatch, a persistent breeze kept whistling. It was
probably through there that, sooner or later, crewmen
would descend and surprise me, curled up in the dark on
what appeared to be a boulder. The time must have been
about nine in the morning; the sun was blazing and the
day very blue above. The boulder that I had slept upon was
no boulder, but a giant turtle.

Heavenly Cargo

I was with a stomach as empty as my soul, observing
the turtle's feet, which resembled old women's hands. The
steamship had a cramped, filthy hold with little room to
move about in. There were trunks, wooden chests, coffers
of tin. At first I thought it might be a passenger steamer.
Not of the Brazilian type, since it had a hold and looked
to be oceangoing, but rather one of those small vessels
that arrive in the area every so often, with diplomatic or
scientific missions aboard. That's why I could be sure it

wasn't a commercial steamer and that its passengers must be special. In the section where the hold tapered toward the bow, I noticed several effigies of saints—life-size. I got up and decided to poke around through the luggage and cargo.

Commerce

The statues of saints were roped together like martyrs. Nearby was a crate filled with smaller statues and statuettes, and additional crates packed with triptychs of the saints, amber rosary beads, crucifixes and tiny tin medals, catechisms bound in mother-of-pearl for first communion, plus countless other articles related to the specifics of Catholic devotion. Several chests contained vestments for mass running the entire gamut of the liturgical year. I discovered cassocks, albs, habits, monstances, crosiers, chalices, cruets, censers, seven-pronged candelabra, hammers with nails, and crowns made of thorns.

Vision

I sat and admired the commercial wisdom of whoever was proprietor of such a body of merchandise. The religious trade would certainly be the most profitable in that territory. All were nominally Catholic. . . . Any backwater colonel would be proud to have a chapel provided with plaster saints and a complete set of vestments on his plantation. And among the store of provisions in his warehouse he would certainly want to include devotional items for the spiritual exercise of his hired hands and their families. I also discovered a stock of wines and guava jam.

Rome

There must have been some two hundred statuettes of St. Anthony alone, in that single crate. And seeing all those vestments brought back to mind the Bishop of Palermo. In 1889, I was in Rome, where the exigencies of Spanish diplomacy had brought me. I was outfitted by the finest tailors and soon got to know Bianca Donatelli, a Tuscan principessa. Rome is an extraordinary city, for all its excesses (everything is lost in the Italian uproar). And Bianca was a blonde with no inhibitions, married to the Marquis de La Froid-Désire. Bianca was also utterly naive about men—a rare woman, indeed. So rare in fact that, defying the basic prejudices of a Catholic country, she had permitted herself to become mistress to a bishop. This before we met one another. The bishop in question was a rancorous Sicilian who, beneath his sweaty cassock, fiercely guarded the hot blood of Palermo. He was a "man of honor," much to my misfortune.

I met Bianca at a Vatican reception. On that same night we took a coach and drove *sulla strada d'Ostia*, experiencing the most exquisite sensations imaginable. Suffice it to say that we spent two days on this trip, until surprised at an inn by my immediate superior: the second undersecretary at the Spanish embassy. The bishop had apparently made threats against my person, and the Spanish ambassador was demanding my immediate presence back at the legation. I left Bianca, only to hear from the ambassador that the bishop could not tolerate the idea of a petty bureaucrat's putting horns on a head (his own, naturally) blessed by the Pope himself. I was transferred to Paris, as third secretary. I confess that I knew very little about Bianca, having heard her say just one single word: *Auguri!* And that only when I was leaving the bedroom, to answer the undersecretary's hysterical knockings at our door.

Piety

I heard a murmur of voices. Up on the quarterdeck a group of women were praying with professional fervor. I felt intrigued to be aboard a steamer transporting such heavenly cargo, together with so many devoted passengers.

Ave Maria!

Through the broken hatch I could glimpse the quarterdeck. I heard a solitary contralto leading an assemblage of limpid voices in unison. With their white habits billowing in the wind, they moved me by their innocence that contrasted in its purity with the yellow river waters. They seemed to be so enthralled that I feel certain, were the steamer to have sunk at that moment, they would all have gone straight to heaven. They were mostly young women, except for two centenarian relics who were uttering their prayers with the whisper of extinct passions. They prayed the entire afternoon, and then when darkness fell the vessel was silenced by the incessant hum of the boilers. I made myself a bed out of vestments, and since it was so terribly hot, I took off my clothes and slept in my undershorts. Let me gently remind the reader that I had boarded this ship in complete formal attire. At any rate, I managed to sleep, but in the middle of the night was wakened by a sudden tempest which shook the boat violently.

Rosary

As I opened my eyes, I found myself staring into a woman's face. I jumped up, shocked and at the same time distressed by the possibility of her raising an outcry. I confess that I'd had just about enough of that hold with its stuffy, liturgical air. But the nun quite simply laughed at me, and I hurriedly attempted to get my pants back on, given that undershorts are not the customary attire with which to meet a sister in the hold of a ship. The nun said hello to me and calmly took a seat on the opposite trunk. We talked quite a bit, and she quickly confessed that she detested saying rosaries at six a.m. and sleeping on coarse linen sheets.

Liturgy

Sister Joana offered to be my accomplice and asked nothing about my past. We were on board a steamship that was in the service of the Catholic Church. A mission of sisters en route to Manaus, where they intended to found a school for orphaned girls. The Bishop of Pará himself was accompanying them. Sister Joana had taken vows two years earlier, and didn't seem too happy about it to me.

Novena

Our rendezvous was to last for nine days, during which time the steamer made port in the following cities: Breves, Piriá, Arumanduba, Almeirim, and Prainha. At each docking, fireworks and open-air mass. . . . The ship was also becoming more and more laden with offerings and donations: cages of chickens, pigs, even cattle. Sister Joana shielded me with her own body, if I may put it that way.

On our first meeting, she told me that she lacked the calling. She had discovered as much, back in Belém, watching an Independence Day parade. All those soldiers.

On the second day she allowed me to give her a kiss, and brought me a plate of chicken ragout.

On the third day she completely disrobed to show me a birthmark in the form of a cross on the side of her left breast. The sign she had mistaken for a calling.

On the other five days she let me explore that not totally feminine, nor masculine body. Joana really did seem to live in another world, but was not a virgin. She told me she had lost her virginity while playing with a cousin. On that first day that we finally made love, she was rather frigid, and I had to practically bruise myself to penetrate that corridor of dried-out walls. She moaned and wanted to scream but was afraid; she felt pain, and through her suffering came to know pleasure. A Christian precept.

The Devil on Board

Just as we were scheduled to begin a new cycle of novenas, we were discovered. Joana had become more and more negligent in her devotion, even slipping away to the hold during hours of communal prayer. The two old relics began to note her absence and, mistrustful of the slightly too terrestrial jubilation which had come to characterize her facial expression, they surprised their stray lamb— *flagrante delicto*—with a stowaway.

Inquisition

The bishop, in his untidy berth, was sweatily preparing for a literal novena, to begin at five that afternoon. He felt a little tired, and his headache was annoying enough to all but extinguish an already tenuous sense of humor (his sermons on perdition were famous in all of Pará, and they say that he knew more than thirty synonyms for the Devil).

The moths, it would seem, had heartily dined on his alb, as well as nibbled a costly rent into the Madeira lace garnishing the cuffs of his vestment. The bishop was trying to adjust the miter on his head, taking the opportunity to assay an expression of pain in the mirror. He noticed a few pimples on his chin, but concluded they were probably due to the spicy cooking on board. He squeezed one by one each of the pimples and his headache began to wane. Until suddenly, he heard the shouts of the nuns outside his cabin and his irritation was rekindled. He thought to himself, annoyed, that the sisters superior must have organized some form of recreation out on deck, at which point the door to his cabin flew open. The two relics entered convulsively.

Exodus

Sister Joana was incarcerated in a cabin and obliged to fast. The sisters superior accused me of playing Satan, to have led a bride of Christ to commit the sin of luxury. I was trying to explain that I didn't see things that way at all, but the bishop—with head pounding—ordered me peremptorily cast ashore. I looked and saw no more than a strip of beach along a barren coast. The bishop, however, seemed to have ears only for the two venerables, as, with richness of detail, they were breathlessly describing the exact circumstances in which they had surprised us.

Correction: with all-encompassing detail (no exaggeration, I promise you), given that one of the two sisters was even able to reproduce certain sounds which caused her mouth to drip with saliva. Émile Zola himself would have envied that naturalistic narrative, and I discovered that through adventure I could easily become a character in Boccaccio's tales.

Flaubertian Chorography

Not very far from the spot where they apparently marooned our hero, the Rio Amazonas is 1.9 kilometers wide and 100 meters deep. It flows at an average speed of 3.8 knots, with between 4 and 12 million cubic meters of water (depending upon the tides) passing every minute. Judging by samples, it is estimated that the amount of soil and other substances dispersed by the water in a single year is close to 620 million tons. Malicious tongues would accuse the same river of a lack of patriotism, given the prodigal way it spills Brazilian soil on the coasts of French Guiana.

Lost Planet

They marooned me on a deserted beach in the Amazonian jungles. And now my adventure begins. . . . I walked along the lonely shore, watching that heavenly vessel paddle off into the distance. I took off my shoes and rolled up my pants. I started kicking at the waves, wandering aimlessly, horrified at the immensity of those yellow waters.

Style

I am the prisoner of a *paysage*. . . . The beach was a no-man's-land, and I began to reflect upon the challenge that such a landscape represented for literature. See how civilized I am? Lost in the jungle but busy pondering literary problems. Problems which, incidentally, I never managed to work out. I only know that such preoccupation with nature effaces human character. And that the Amazonian landscape is so complex in its detail that, inevitably, we are led to victimize its contours with sonorous-sounding adjectives, sacrificing the real in all its grandeur.

Pitfalls

Today, old and tired, what can I say of that landscape? After one or two adjectives, I feel most at home with the chaotic enumeration of the avant-garde, symptom of Amazonian megalomania. Within those two thousand square meters of jungle around me, I could have found close to five hundred species of plant life alone. Thousands of kilos of variegated leaves, tons of trunks, countless roots . . . more organic matter than the mountains and rocks of my native land. Over 840 kilos of biological substance is massed in a single hectare of jungle. The Amazon is putrid but alive. I was hungry, and thinking at that moment of trying to find something to eat. Some kind of fruit, perhaps. I stopped, though, fearful of poisoning myself.

Prehistoric

It began to get dark and I watched the sky over the jungle transform into a vast rotunda of stars. What did *parvenus* or prima donnas, *cocottes* or vagabonds, priests, diplomats, or fools have to do with that infinite wall of green leaves, with no discernible beauty whatsoever? Someone in Belém once told me that you become mute in the face of the Amazonian setting. Not so . . . you become humiliated, by the blinding intuition of absolute prehistory. An experience which made me feel profoundly uneasy. As a son of the sea of Cádiz, I had already known the crushing power of nature. But the sea is classical—implacable perhaps, but without obfuscation. The jungle is reticent, Muslim: no tides, no waves, no sun on the back of emeralds and foam. What I saw in the twilight was an immense Persian carpet.

Syntax

Out of sheer inertness, I sat down in the sand and let the landscape invade the action. My look was a figure of speech.

Jules Verne

The seat of my trousers was soaking wet from sitting on the beach, and I realized that the position of adventurer is almost always an uncomfortable one. The adventurer seems to live as if he were constantly in midcareer. Dotage is nonexistent, and any contretemps are always penciled out of adventure stories. Well, let me tell you, no one has it harder than an adventurer. If only I were some Phileas Fogg, out in the channel of the river there, taking my voyage around the world in eighty easy rubber plantations.

Phileas Fogg

I had no fears of wild beasts, and knew perfectly well that bizarre situations are also aspects of reality. Robinson Crusoe, the brevity of life is far worse than an attack of pirates.

Materialism

By morning I discovered that the world doesn't merit quite so much analysis once your empty stomach starts twisting for some action. The insects and animals made a hell of a racket during the night; I barely slept a wink. Looking around, I found a few inga fruits.

Gulliver

A storm was coming up, when I suddenly heard a noise on the river—the sound of oars approaching. I was overjoyed, thinking it might be river folk on their way to some get-together or other. Prudently, though, I still preferred to check my enthusiasm and hide myself. An adventurer in the bush is worth any number caught red-handed. . . . A cold chill crept up my spine as I realized they were actually savages! I was hidden up in a tall tree, whence I spotted some ten dugouts, loaded with Indians exaggeratedly happy to be sitting with priests and nuns. They disembarked and led the servants of God to the beach, as if they were precious cargo. And that they were. . . . The Indians settled their guests upon an elevation of sand, and I saw that some of the nuns were crying. The savage in charge of the war party was gesticulating to the bishop and saying something, but the bishop answered nothing and simply knelt in the resigned prayer of a benign martyr. A few other savages were busy improvising makeshift grills with tree branches, foraging in the nearby jungle. I held my breath as they walked back and forth underneath me. They could easily have caught a glimpse of me up in the tree. It took them the remainder of the day to set up the grills and prepare the pyres.

Ethnography I

The victims were tied to trunks by a long tether which permitted them a certain amount of movement. Taking advantage of the respite, the servants of God knelt together to pray. Afterward, the Indians offered them cudgels so that they might defend themselves. The victims refused, and it was with indignation that the savages were reduced to splattering their brains through the air with masterly strokes. The bodies were immediately undressed and dismembered. With no visible seasoning, they were spitted to be roasted.

Ethnographer

A few inga fruits were hardly enough to fill a stomach, and that sweetish odor of roasting meat was tempting. I don't wish to horrify anyone, and it's difficult to surmise whether I would have participated in such a banquet had I been invited to. But my hunger was certainly fierce, of that there's no denying. The sweat, meanwhile, was pouring from my armpits.

Ethnography II

The savages were rinsing their throats with a drink that must have been alcoholic. Each round of drink augmented their euphoria, as they danced obliviously around the bonfires. And I was with both arms numb from hugging to the limb of my tree for so long. My legs were reduced to pins and needles, and I shut my eyes with pain. Then I opened them, only to see a few of the Indians tying a nun to a tree, apparently for a little fun with bows and arrows. The nun was Joana. . . .

Forgive Me, Reader!

Once again I seem to be obliged to interrupt this narrative. In 1898, there were no Indians left on the banks of the lower Amazon. And since the early eighteenth century there had been no further reports of cannibalism in the region. No white man, at least by oral means, had been digested in the nineteenth century. Our hero was evidently trying to add a little local color to those uneventful days he spent in Santarém, where—together with Joana, the nun without religious vocation—he was actually set ashore. In Santarém, he ran into an English scientific expedition and immediately struck up a friendship with the expedition's head, Dr. Henry Lust, the great naturalist and gastronome. Our hero will yet have things to say about this curious subject of Her Majesty.

Geography

The Rio Amazonas, coursing as it does through a vast savannah basin, has a sluggish current and produces sinuous trajectories. It is the largest hydrographic basin in the world and the only one that has not bequeathed an important civilization to the history of man. They say that the Amazonas is not a river . . . it's a geological *gaffe*.

Discovery

I awoke with the lazy light of morning dominating the beach, which the savages had already abandoned. I slid down the tree, dropping to the sand exhausted, only to feel the intense heat. Suddenly I heard a soft murmuring of prayers and stood up frightened. Joana was still tied up, her habit soiled like bird feathers. I ran to her assistance, tugging at the thick liana vines until my fingers began to bleed. Joana came to in a semi-delirious state and began to struggle with me. I had to look for something sharp to slash the vines away, and at last came across a wooden knife left behind by the Indians. Joana fell into my arms nearly unconscious and pleaded for water. I arranged a makeshift bed of leaves and laid my companion down there, while she did little more than move her head insentiently.

Insomnia

A terrible night. . . . Afraid to leave Joana in that bed of leaves, I decided to carry her up into the tree with me. Then I couldn't allow myself to sleep, for fear she might slip and plunge to her death.

Survival in the Jungle

We spent three days of rain, and I had improvised a covert for our protection. I was growing desperate with Joana's frail condition, so I began to forage for food in the nearby jungle. On the second day I managed to kill a heron. It was standing immobile in a pool of water, and I took full advantage of its ignorance as to human intentions. Joana finally began to recover her spirits a little, but now gave herself up to prayer. To me, the Devil seemed to be the heat and humidity. The biceps in my legs were practically devoured by insects.

Lost and Found

I think it must have been the fifth or sixth day, I no longer remember. . . . I looked to my side and saw that Joana had vanished. I was too tired and defeated even to contemplate trying to find her. But when I went down to the beach I discovered that she was there, gently splashing the water with her foot. She seemed better, and it struck me that she shared a certain affinity with that heron: her slender silhouette, the soiled habit lifted to keep it dry, and a face with its tawny complexion, shimmering in the agitation of waters at her feet. She saw me and let a few tears run down her cheeks.

Confessions

Joana had still not reconciled herself. She confided that she wanted to return to a convent. She had gotten it into her head that this tragedy had been an additional sign. One night, however, she kissed me and compelled me to run my hand over her body. She masturbated with my fingers and cried afterward. I don't know why I began to tell her the story of the tears of Agnès Louise La Fontaine. Tears quite at variance with those that Joana was shedding at the moment.

Sexual Revolution

Paris, 1891. The City of Lights was being shaken by anarchistic attempts at assassination. The Place Pigalle had been invaded by prostitutes from Algiers. The Théâtre du Chatelet announced the debut of a Spanish singer, and it was there that I met Agnès Louise. She was a friend of Jean Paul, the young anarchist who frequented my home. She turned out to be quite an admirable woman—like all women in the past of any man. She was also the complete sexual realization of industrial France. We began to meet at a hotel on the Rue de Rivoli, near the Louvre. In that hotel bedroom I received expert lessons in what France has always known best how to export. Agnès was truly unselfish, and while she was providing me with a veritable doctoral thesis on the erogenous zones, we were surprised by her husband. I've never had luck with husbands and we took a few shots our way. Fortunately, the husband had a terrible aim and suffered from convulsions. I watched him succumb to a fit of coughing that nearly asphyxiated him, as if his own organic putrefaction were a direct result of the corrupting influence of his wife. We came to the rescue of the poor shipowner, and I gained another transfer. Agnès did not fail to give me an unforgettable send-off at Bordeaux, however.

Tempest

Wind and rain washed away our little covert. We were cast into the open storm, soaked to the skin, stiff with cold. It's incredible how cold it gets in an Amazonian rainstorm. The tempest lasted throughout the night, and in the morning we were greeted by a dreamlike vision. A steamship was navigating close to the beach. It was flying an English flag. We couldn't believe our eyes. The rain was much lighter now and sweeping the beach like a soft curtain. We ran to our salvation. . . .

Hail, Science!

Sir Henry Lust welcomed us aboard with his portly carriage and blond mustache of a British officer. He smelled of snuff, a habit he had picked up while in India. He proved to be a scientist visiting the Amazonian plains at the invitation of the Brazilian government. He was on his way back to Manaus, where he intended to terminate his voyage of research and return to London.

Tea and Sympathy

They gave us dry clothes and a warm cabin. My body was feverish and my eyes were burning. I felt the steamer put off again, while the sun began to open up a blue patch of sky. Joana was in a deep slumber, her body wrapped in blankets in the berth. I tried to get some rest myself. Toward the end of the afternoon, the first mate came to announce that Sir Henry wished the pleasure of our company on deck for tea. I led Joana, still groggy with sleep, to the quarterdeck and was surprised to find it transformed into an agreeable salon for refreshments, where even waterproof curtains had been lowered on the sides. We sat at Sir Henry's table, and I helped myself to some delicious crackers which melted on contact with a cup of aromatic India tea. Other tables began to be taken, apparently by the various members of the expedition. At one of them, however, sat an elegant woman whose face was hidden behind a dark veil. She was attended by three young ladies who acted as maids-of-honor.

Drama

The elegant woman was Justine L'Amour, prima donna of La Compagnie Opératique de la France. And François Blangis, the concert master, soon showed up to sip his tea with delicate slices of chocolate cake. What could a troupe of *artistes* be doing on a scientific expedition? Good question to close another chapter of a *feuilleton*.

Extraterrestrial Natives in the Amazon?

Sir Henry Lust was in the Amazon at his own expense, though with the permission of the Brazilian authorities. He was a rich man, to be sure, in spite of his twenty-eight years. Sir Henry was an engineer, and when in Bombay, had founded the British Society for Primitive Metaphysical Research. He spoke in the first-person plural and had received the Order of the White Eagle of Addis Ababa. He was one of those pioneer spirits who explored the Amazon for the sake of science.

After swallowing a few light biscuits, Sir Henry offered me his learned theories: "If they should try to tell you in Manaus," Sir Henry grunted, "that the Amazonas Theater was actually the work of an obscure former governor, you mustn't pay the slightest attention. Sheer rubbish. The fruit of native ignorance, I dare say. No, Mr. Aria, we are quite certain that extraterrestrial beings had a hand in the matter and that the Amazonas Theater is a sterling example of their existence. Our concept of the Amazonas Theater as an artifact from space is a purely rational one; which is to say, this manifest intervention in the heart of the equatorial jungle must be a product of intelligent forces, more powerful than ourselves, but material beings nonetheless—in short, inhabitants of exterior space." Sir Henry punctuated his final phrase by pointing a white finger, yellowed from smoke, at a blue sky. The wines of Sir Henry, however, were quite worthy of extraterrestrials.

Rupestrian Painting

"It all began in the spring of '97, Mr. Aria, when we were on our visit to the caves of Altamira. As we carefully perused that reliquary of rock painting, we were struck by the curiousness of a design which had gone unperceived in its true detail until that moment." (Sir Henry was a formidable Amazonologist. He was thoroughly versed in the works of La Condamine and Humbolt, and considered the Amazon an ideal spot for the cultivation of palm trees.) "We sensed immediately that we were on the verge of a smashing discovery. Within the perimeters of that crudely wrought design we could clearly glimpse a winged and flaming artifact whose silhouette was identical to that of the Amazonas Theater. We carefully reproduced the design inside our Baedecker and isolated ourself for fifteen months at the London archives, where we accumulated more than nine hundred pages of painstaking annotation. We are now corroborating our findings, and have already conducted on-the-spot investigations throughout the intricate corridors of the Amazonas Theater itself."

Physical Anthropology

Sir Henry could not conceive of the Teatro Amazonas as the work of any human force. Much less the product of semicivilized natives, notorious for their racial inferiority and total incapacity for logical ratiocination.

Márcio Souza

Colonial Erudition

According to the Carmelite Montserrat, in his *Marvelous Description of the River of Amazonas During the Just War of Marañon*, written in 1665, a native who had been taught to read and write actually suffered cerebral convulsions which proved fatal when attempting to read the *Summa* of Thomas Aquinas.

Delacroix

Justine L'Amour repeatedly wrung her hands moist with sweat, borrowing a nervous theatrical gesture. Her companions believed that she was on the brink of total collapse. She spoke little, broke every glass she held in her hand, and cried continually. I felt truly distressed by the deplorable state of that wretched diva and didn't resist for very long the temptation to learn the source of her grief. Justine L'Amour, languishing on the quarterdeck like some ragged Charlotte Corday.

Native Greetings

We were passing the town of Óbidos, and its cluster of houses came alive with the breathless curiosity of the townspeople. Children were running along the high banks, and a group of elders, standing in the mouth of one of those huge dockside warehouses, began to wave to us. Sir Henry ordered our steamer to blow a few strident whistles of fraternization.

Operatic Tribulations

Here is what Blangis told me: "On opening night everything seemed fine. We had rehearsed until five in the afternoon, the orchestra was properly tuned, and the cast appeared to be in perfect form. It would be our tenth performance of *Aida*. The scenery was all set up, and we ate backstage as we always did on opening nights. We were nervous, of course, which was only natural. After all, it was to be our first recital in Brazil, and we had no idea what our audience would be like. Half an hour before the curtain went up, the performance was already sold out, so we hoped for at least a genteel public. Justine was looking lovely as a goddess, and from the box office we heard the good news that we would collect a handsome sum. The first act proceeded without interruption, save the two ovations before the end of the act. The Brazilians appeared to be quite refined, and our spirits rose."

Caribbean Casualties

Blangis' fears were not motivated by any anti-Brazilian sentiments. In Cayenne, the colonial administration had taxed the opera as an article of luxury, which nearly bankrupted the troupe. In Trinidad-Tobago, they got arrested as Irish terrorists. In Havana, two members of the chorus were raped.

Bel Canto Equivocations

Blangis still: "The final duet between Radamès and Aida was already underway when we heard the scream of a woman in the audience." (I felt a hot flash of shame rush through my body.) "An altercation ensued, out in the auditorium, and then we watched the stage itself being suddenly invaded by the civil guard. We became desperate, thinking we were being arrested again. Robert, the set designer, rushed over to ask me if operatic sets were actually permitted in Brazil. I didn't know what to answer, given that human customs vary from latitude to latitude. Meanwhile our troupe had entered the foray, battling the soldiers bravely, but unfortunately, we were greatly outnumbered."

Paris Match

Blangis had read the story of a French explorer who had been put to death at the hands of some African tribe, for the simple act of having sneezed in front of their women. An enthusiastic devotee of snuff, the explorer couldn't resist a healthy sneeze or two before the indignant gaze of the blacks. For those heathens, apparently, to sneeze in the presence of women was a crime as nefarious as fornicating on the altar of a church. Who was to say if the opera didn't possess some taboo in the Amazon?

Prima Donna

Without courage to face the future, Justine was offended by Blangis' apparent indifference. I suspected she might well be consoling herself in the arms of the redoubtable Sir Henry.

To the Dungeon

Blangis: "They wouldn't even permit us to remove our makeup, and so our ragged band of bruised Egyptians were escorted through the streets by militiamen, like fugitives from a Mardi Gras. The central headquarters of the Paraensian police department is the most infected pesthole I have ever seen. They threw us into a damp cell, stinking of urine. There were more than twenty men squeezed into a circular cubicle of some four meters in diameter. We had to take shifts in order to sleep, and spent the entire day without food or water. The women had been taken up to a room on the second floor. I was so desperate— without an inkling as to what to attribute our imprisonment—that I gave an absurd deposition. Three hours of brutal interrogation cleared up nothing for me. And they tore up in my face the certificate from the governor permitting us to perform *Aida*."

THE EMPEROR OF THE AMAZON

Diplomacy

The French consul general, M. Dupont, threatened to break diplomatic relations with Brazil if the commissioner of police did not allow him to see the detained French citizens immediately. The commissioner answered that he didn't give a solemn shit about the Third Republic of France. He had orders from higher up.

Metropolitan Headlines

The *Jornal do Brasil*, in Rio de Janeiro, announced that, in the state of Pará, an opera company of Belgian nationality was being held incommunicado until the diva of the troupe should give herself to the prefect of police.

Tropical Medicine

GALVEZ: So the company disbanded?

BLANGIS: We spent twenty days in the *bastille*, by which time only four girls were left.

GALVEZ: The others deserted?

BLANGIS: A few; the worst was *le mal tropique*, which took most of them into the next world.

GALVEZ: *Le mal tropique*?

BLANGIS: *La fièvre jaune* . . . yellow fever! The medical examiner insisted that we must have picked it up in Cayenne. But as far as I'm concerned it was the lack of hygienic conditions—we were forced to sleep in our own feces! *Vraiment terrible!*

Troisième République

M. Dupont finally managed to liberate the *bastille*, by bribing the commissioner of police with a case of champagne. Sir Henry Lust, devotee of the arts, agreed to transport the survivors to Manaus, where they would try to begin a new life. Robert Boulingrin, the set designer, went to work for the Paraensian Power & Light Company.

Calderón de la Barca

I offered to organize a *zarzuela* act with the remnants
of the former company. After all, I felt to a certain extent
guilty about their plight. So I stepped into the variety
lights through the gates of remorse, a very Spanish gate.
Sir Henry approved of the idea, promising to help. He
had connections in Manaus and was a friend of the proprietor of the Hotel Cassina, a luxurious hostelry for adventurers. Blangis baptized the new company *Les Comédiens Tropicals*.

Showboat

I organized a variety act then with a tableau in homage
to the Paraguayan War, always a great success in the
Amazon. We started rehearsals aboard, alternating with
scientific lectures given by Sir Henry. The ship was navigating the waters of Utopia.

Zarzuela

There turned out to be a small orchestra on board. The
first mate played the bassoon; the steward, guitar; the cook,
violoncello; and Blangis, the concertina. Justine L'Amour
was to begin with a monologue from Molière's *Les Pré-
cieuse Ridicules*. The show would end with Blangis, as the
Brazilian Duke of Caxias, singing a ballad of my own
composition to the music of Rossini. Very patriotic-
sounding. . . .

First Lecture

"We categorically reject that traditional science so fearful of the imagination. We look forward to a new science,
totally liberated from the shackles of Judeo-Christian ra-
tionalism. The mysterious *art-nouveau* monument referred
to as the Amazonas Theater, in Brazil, is actually an
enormous architectonic complex, precisely structured, more

than one hundred feet in length, and weighing thousands of tons. It was erected at a distance of nine hundred miles from the Atlantic Ocean, above the line of the equator. Most intriguing is the gilded cupola that crowns this monumental edifice lost in the tropical jungle. To transport only this cupola, a force equivalent to the strength of forty thousand men would have been required.

"For us, the key to this megalithic colossus lies in the oral legends of the natives, which speak of a powerful "Master" known as Jurupari, subjugator of women, who traveled to Earth from exterior space—more precisely, from the Pleiades, in the constellation of Taurus, the Bull. Given the technical impossibility of a megalithic civilization's having had the capacity to produce so complicated a monument in the midst of the tropical wilds, on a plateau that clearly resembles a landing port for space vehicles, we emphatically deny to the architects of latex—who moreover do not possess the technological sophistication—the feat of realizing such an undertaking. The idea that the Amazonas Theater dates from a recent epoch is utterly ridiculous, a pack of nonsense on the part of sheer duffers. We have conducted exhaustive tests with samples, at the Institute of Nuclear Metaphysics in Addis Ababa, which reveal a period of—at the very least—a million years ago, placing the advent of the structure somewhere back in the Glacial Era.

"Upon examining the edifice, some six months ago, we were able to note the presence of a variety of human remains in the back of the stage area—mummified remains. But we are not dealing with a funereal monument, though we cannot discount the hypothesis of a possible cultural tomb. Clearly, however, what can be affirmed is the existence of biocosmic forces yet to be discovered.

"The Amazonas Theater represents, to our way of thinking, the most perfect indication of the presence of extraterrestrial beings on Earth after the pyramids of Egypt and the megalopolis of Tiahuanaco. What surprises us, however, is the cautious dissimulation of its true purpose, on the one hand; and *art nouveau* as a legacy on an extraterrestrial civilization, bequeathed by Jurupari, the voyager of the Pleiades, who one day soared to Earth in a flaming cupola, impregnating native women, on the other."

Molière

Justine was divine with that monologue. She confessed to me, however, that she was doing it more out of solidarity, since she felt debased by being compelled to enact declamatory theater. A courageous woman. . . . We would rehearse until one in the morning, and now Joana, with her tawny skin and dark eyes, began to appear more and more without the drapery of her habit. Much closer to the world in that yellow close-fitting dress.

Cervantes

Ambling about on deck, I began to think of those lines from *Galatea* and my "fugitive abode." Joana told me that she still felt a little ashamed to be walking around without her habit. Apparently for that reason she crossed her arms quite a bit.

Happy New Year

We commemorated the advent of the new year, anchored in the city of Parintins, already in the state of Amazonas. There was a sandbar, right at the entrance to the harbor, where young girls would sun themselves. Sir Henry organized a little celebration for us all, and we had a visit from the Mayor of Parintins. We drank *jerez* and, at midnight, when we brought in the year 1899, Sir Henry danced with Justine L'Amour in honor of Her Majesty.

Inspiration

At lunchtime, Blangis entertained us with a few feats of magic. He cleaned out Sir Henry's pockets without the latter's feeling it and plucked sixpence from the nose of the waiter. I added the number to our zarzuela.

THE EMPEROR OF THE AMAZON

Second Lecture

"We find traces of descriptions of the Amazonas Theater in the *Epic of Gilgamesh*, in the *Egyptian Book of the Dead*, and in the *Centuries* of Nostradamus. To take but one example, in the *Popol-Vul* (sacred text of the Mayas) the god of mediocrity, Tarzenclar, descends on a winged artifact designated Theantlokk Amargzanoacal, whose cupola of sulfuric transformations shines like gold. We are also reminded of the winged chariot that transported the prophet Ezekiel.

"While engaged in our researches among the peasants of Altamira, we encountered a legend that designates the image within the grotto as the *Égida del Amazonas,* or literally the Aegis of Amazonas, from the Greek word *Aigis*, meaning 'cloud': tempestuous cloud that permits of travel. From which we rationally deduce that the Aegis of Amazonas is nothing less than a winged artifact, vehicle for cosmic travel, used by evolved creatures stemming from the remote past.

"Observing photographic plates of the Amazonas Theater, we can admire the diversity of composition reflected in the nave, the bizarre cupola which is obviously its generative center, the supporting pillars, and the myriad sculptures suggesting exotic figures similar to the extraterrestrials in question. As for the nature of the external colorations of our monument, we have recorded a gradual change effected throughout the centuries. In the beginning of its history, it must have been quite metallic and shiny, this according to the chronicles of Spanish explorers from the sixteenth century. Fray Hernando de Linhares would have been eclipsed by the brilliance of the monument. But with the passage of time the nave has cooled down, gradually turning to a rose color. I predict that it will eventually freeze at a bureaucratic gray.

"Our dear friend, Elizabeth Agassis, confessed to us recently that the area was taboo as late as 1865; ships would not permit of any access to the colossus. Elizabeth, however, curious as ever, slipped past the blockade and witnessed, at great personal peril, an extraordinary spectacle: brilliant lights revolving about the cupola on a dark night. Elizabeth Agassis did not include this experience in her *Voyage to Brazil*, fearing reprisals from skeptics. But she readily confessed to us privately that a native had shown her the mouth of a tunnel that actually linked the monument to the monastery of the Dalai Lama, in Tibet. We have not yet managed to locate this tunnel, but as long as a more than cursory examination remains to be undertaken, meter by precious meter, throughout the sinuous confines of the Amazonas Theater, one dare not deny *a priori* the existence of a galactic culture of staggering proportions still operative in the Amazon."

Scientific Praxis

Justine L'Amour was no longer to be glimpsed wearing the tragical mask of a protagonist from Racine. Sir Henry's treatments were effecting a marvelous cure upon the ex-diva. Obviously she must have been experiencing a few cosmic surprises in the cabin of my illustrious host. Sir Henry, after all, was also a member of the famous Hellfire Club.

Rational Conclusion

If we refuse to believe in a temple set down in the jungle—or in the narratives of the savages, ever inclined to legends—one nevertheless has to admire the hero Jurupari and his chariot of fire, endlessly seducing Indian virgins with a mysterious sexual technique. Sir Henry had catalogued a legend that described the sexual organ of Jurupari as a species of magic flute. I believe that the erotic secret of Jurupari was known to Sir Henry. . . . I believe that one does not lift a prima donna out of her apathy without a heavenly foundation in technique. . . .

Fieldwork

Our trip was rather long because at every embankment of rock the steamship would be forced to anchor. Sir Henry wanted to debark and inspect the designs engraved by long-forgotten hands. In Itacoatiara, which means "Painted Stone," we spent three entire days. Sir Henry collected a vast number of inscriptions there, while we collected—from the natives—a couple of turtles and a pirarucu (a kind of gigantic salmon).

More Proofs

Sir Henry passed a night dreaming about the images at Itacoatiara. In his dream, the figure of a completely undressed man, with noble features, let himself be caressed by beautiful jungle maidens. The apparition professed to him in a voice of ejaculation that the inscriptions on the stones actually contained prophecies. I was never able to verify whether at some later date Sir Henry managed to translate the meaning of those designs, but he did confess to me that he had experienced a sexual discharge on the night in question.

Anniversary Cake

The 20th of February. My second anniversary in Brazil. . . . We had been voyaging with Sir Henry since December. We commemorated the occasion with glasses of champagne and a chocolate cake molded in the shape of the Teatro Amazonas. The work of Sir Henry's ingenious chef. . . . We began exchanging notions concerning the mysteries of the heavens, a specialty among Spaniards. Sir Henry, in the middle of our conversation, asked me if I were capable of cleansing honor with blood.

Tragedy in the Pampas

1896, in Buenos Aires: I wash my honor with spilled blood, and then some. I had been transferred to Buenos Aires, only to discover how much I liked that city with its curious combination of European tradition and thoroughly British climate. Then one day, while attending a horse race at the Jockey Club, I felt my eyes drawn to a white and delicate luster—the bust of Maria Isabel y Fierro, nearly bouncing from her undisciplined décolletage with the impertinence of unplucked delicacies—where I gleaned delights warm enough to melt any etymological "iron," even from a name like Fierro, into churning butter. Don Ramon Lizando y Aragon y Fierro, Isabel's father, did not deserve to be the author of such a work of art. He was busy dreaming up a marriage for Isabel that would simply allow him to increase his immense fiefdom. *El Toro Loco,* as he was known to his cronies, set sparks flying when he learned that his only Isabel was no longer an innocent maid. I had stained the honor of the house of Fierro and would pay for blood with blood.

Duel in Ezeiza

Pablo, Isabel's brother, challenged me to a duel, a practice illegal in Argentina, but widely invoked nonetheless among men of society. I cut Pablo down with a single shot, among the trees in the forest of Ezeiza. Staring down at the bloodstain on the grass, I thought to myself, while the seconds of the dead man carried away his corpse, that this was the second time in less than a month that I had shed Fierro blood for motives of passion. I was summarily dismissed from the Spanish diplomatic service and received the invitation to leave Argentina within forty-eight hours.

Happiness

Justine L'Amour was in such gay spirits that I decided to include a cancan in our zarzuela. The following morning we were to arrive in Manaus. Joana felt nervous, but at the same time anxious to arrive. She originally came from the capital, and her parents still lived there. It was Joana who had told me that, for the people of Amazonas, the Teatro Amazonas would stand forever as a symbol.

Tradition

The Isle of Marapatá, where adventurers were accustomed to lay aside their conscience before entering the foray. I seemed to be the only adventurer to enter Manaus with my conscience intact. Something I never regretted.

PART THREE

*March through June,
Manaus,
in the Year of 1899*

*Not a fruit of every climate, liberty in the Amazonas isn't
the easiest thing to grow.*

—Luiz Galvez

Zarzuela

Not as well known a phenomenon as it should be, the true nature of the Amazonian delirium at the very height of the rubber boom perhaps defies ordinary description. Yet if for now one finds it relegated to the realm of *feuilleton* and the dreams of poets, there is no doubt that one day it will find its way into the pages of Brazilian history. Then, would to heaven it not be for the enrichment of some "Brazilianist" abroad, since right here we have men enough capable of the truth—as soon as the law permits.

Offenbach

Pink line of corpulent flesh, reminding me of my forty years of age. Justine L'Amour's legs sparkling in black-and-silver lace stockings. Lights aglow, in this simulacrum of a metropolis. *Les Comédiens Tropicals* shifting to the back of a tiny stage. Blangis in a white beard and gold-trimmed galoons, flanked by *papier-mâché* angels, virtuously raising his sword. A solitary *pizzicato* from a violin, and my exaggerated sigh. The percussion's slow crescendo, suddenly silenced. Everyone electrified by another performance. . . . Applause!

Culture

I was leaning against the door that led to the dressing room, well in the back of the salon. I smiled and joined in the applause. Another evening of unexpected receipts, our second week of success. The *Theater News*, the showbiz weekly of Manaus, had classified our spectacular as "First-rate!" The orchestra under the direction of the intrepid "maestro" Chiquinho Gonzaga—also known as Chico Clap, by virtue of his chronic venereal infection—was, at the very least, infernal with its fifteen supernumeraries.

Box Office

Sir Henry continued on to São Gabriel da Cachoeira, where he would hopefully attend a ceremony dedicated to Jurupari, among the Tukano tribe, and thus pursue his researches. The zarzuela was drawing a handsome return each week, and nothing seemed to please Justine more than her balance in the London Bank.

Social Problem

We had spent, by now, two weeks in Manaus. The reader must already have gathered that this is a linear story. My French friends had disembarked in the most disconsolate anonymity, wasting away for an entire morning in the pestilential harborage of outriggers and prostitutes. Blangis eventually managed to find an inn with cold-water baths and a price modest enough to permit at least a fortnight of food and shelter. I had taken a conveyance with Joana, leaving Justine sitting among suitcases and trunks (they had managed to retrieve a good part of their wardrobe from the fiasco in Belém). The French girls stood sweating among peddlers, sailors, gentlemen in *sakkos*, black Barbadians, and passersby with aboriginal features.

Apprehensiveness of a Prima Donna

Justine was fearful that Blangis, in possession of the receipts, might be tempted to buy some rubber plantation about to be liquidated.

Palatine Prestige

At the Government Palace I had the good fortune to meet the journalist Thaumaturgo Vaez. I spoke about the situation of the French *artistes* and mentioned our zarzuela. It turned out that Vaez was *the* man in Manaus. He took me over to the Hotel Cassina, where we had a talk with the proprietor. The recommendation of Sir Henry also weighed heavily, so it was immediately decided that the French Comédiens would have their debut at the hotel, following the engagement of a pair of Spanish dancers.

Credit

I dropped in at the London Bank, only to discover that Cira had sent me some additional funds. Vaez took me over to the Old England Shop, where I bought myself some new clothes. A linen shirt cost more than fifty dollars. And, in those days, let me tell you. . . .

Soul of Andalusia

The Spaniards at the Hotel Cassina held no Spanish passports. They were dyed-in-the-wool Brazilians, from Recife, and disappointing. Conchita (with a name like that, who could be from Spain?) apparently refused to yield to any unseemly approaches, and Pablo (in fact, Paulo da Silva) knew well enough how to temper, with those muscles of his, any spectators overly enamored with the lovely ankles of that *bailadora* (pseudo) *sevillana*. The tastes of the Hotel Cassina were fairly materialistic, in fact.

The Aesthetics of Taste

In the Amazonas, whenever the public did not sympathize with the performance—or were overly sympathetic to an excessive degree—they tended to be rather hot-blooded. Blangis, well aware of that, would go on stage with half a bottle of gin under his belt. He said it was simply to counteract the preponderant odors of patchouli and Lublin toilet water in the audience, trying to keep his girls ignorant of the psychological nuances of their public.

Public Notice

On the wall of the Hotel Cassina, a charming public notice:

PROHIBITED
*The Use of Revolvers, Bow & Arrows, or Cold Steel
Anywhere on These Premises
DECREE N°. 38
Commissioner of Public Safety*

Generosity

Justine began to receive baskets of flowers, expensive drinks, and even more expensive jewelry. Yet she swore that she had not conceded any greater favors than an occasional osculation for friendship's sake. Les Comédiens Tropicals were already put up at the Hotel Cassina itself.

Professionalism

The zarzuela was rehearsed daily. I was never present, going out in the morning and only returning to the hotel in time for the show. My friend Thaumaturgo Vaez gradually introduced me to this odd society of millionaires. Vaez himself was a fascinating, appealing fellow. In those few days he had already insinuated his way into my life like an old and comfortable friend. He insisted I come stay at his house, a veritable chateau out on the edge of town in the Cachoeirinha section, complete with an orchard full of delicious tropical fruit. He was also editor of the newspaper *Jornal do Comércio*, where he wrote, among other things, an extremely popular column of limericks and light verse, in which he would deftly register the more thrilling events of the day with gentle quips and irony.

Journalism

About our variety show he wrote:

> From far-off France you came,
> Bringing art's welcome light,
> And with skillful song and dance,
> You seduced me . . . how deny it?
> Oh, graceful nymphs and dryads,
> In your beauteous artifice!

Progress

There are over 35,000 uses for rubber; yet it remains nevertheless—according to Henry Ford—an industry still in its infancy.

Traditional Values

The applause continued every night, and afterward the girls would quickly change clothes, eager to return to the salon and the conviviality of their newfound friends. On the piano, tangos and maxixes. Meanwhile, I would sit with Vaez at a table always reserved for us, in close proximity to a fan. Then, one night, in walked the most controversial figure in all of Manaus, Colonel Eduardo Ribeiro. He respectfully kissed the hand of each of the girls present and piped down Vaez with a gesture that amounted to an order.

Modesty

VAEZ: Colonel Eduardo Ribeiro is the man principally responsible for the beauty of our city. His governorship is now a part of history, but it was he who transformed Manaus into a truly civilized place to live.

RIBEIRO: Enough of that fancy prose, Thaumaturgo. Let's order some drinks, which is more to the point. Manaus, civilized . . . only a poet!

At a Glance

I tugged at my stiff collar and glimpsed Justine, so perfectly at home in that salon full of liquor and strong cigars.

The Theater News

"Well, dear readers, what have we here? The Gallic Comédiens performing nightly at the Hotel Cassina seem to have become the rave of the entire city. Even respectable ladies have begun to be seen there, not to mention a certain canon who found himself inexplicably in attendance last Tuesday. And was that the muffled thunder of Olympus itself we heard rumbling over in a corner?"

Amazonian Winter

Thirty degrees Celsius. Watermarks evaporating from the walls like pale relics of the bygone rains. I was staring out the window at the busy thoroughfare, streetcars crossing the wine-colored cobbles. Women wearing extravagant hats, strolling arm and arm with their consorts. A city coruscated by electricity. Victorian architecture, or Manueline? An unfinished church, and a beach of putrid mud. I had spent a month in Manaus, without incident.

Metaphysics

April 1899. I received an insistent invitation from the Secretary of the Public Treasury, Major Freire, to come to a séance at his mansion. The invitation also stipulated that I bring Justine along. Whatever actually took place at those sessions was such a well-guarded secret that, around the hearth, it could only be discussed in half-whispers, out of earshot of young ladies and children. Finally, a little action. . . .

Conan Doyle

Justine accompanied me in an eye-filling low-cut dress. She knew well enough how to be agreeable when she wanted to. At Freire's house a gramophone was crackling with "*C'era una volta un principe*," by Carlos Gomes. English chairs and heavy drapes promised an emotional evening. The major seemed intent upon uniting Alan Kardec with the *Kama Sutra*. The solitude of Manaus led money to seek a metaphysics in the other extreme. The *nouveaux riches* also had to have their spirituality. Convinced that Manaus was the most isolated city in the West, they sought to encounter some mystery. The major confessed to me that he dreaded decadence, and then recalled the Spanish Main of Arab sacrifice.

Berlitz School

FREIRE: *Celà peut paraître drôle, mais moi, j'ai besoin de civilisation.*
GALVEZ: *Vous avez reçu une très mauvaise éducation, mon cher Freire.*
JUSTINE: *Moi, j'ai peur. . . .*

Omar Khayyam

Murmured phrases and, in the mirror, the smoke from a fervently sucked nargileh. People spread about on easy chairs and velvet ottomans. I could smell the sweet scent of hashish, and eyes glowed like dry leaves consumed by a slow-burning fire. Someone observed to Justine that his fingers were numb. It was Eduardo Ribeiro, in need of a light for the cigarillo protruding from his lips. Justine opened her purse, took out a box of matches, and lacerated the darkness with light. Ribeiro thanked her in that agreeable haze of mellifluous bhang. I saw the two take one another's hand and make their way over to a sofa that lay on the far side of the living room like some lost leather horizon.

The Collector

I was standing and watched Ribeiro slip his arm around Justine's shoulder. She smiled and permitted him to explore those evident breasts of hers. Ribeiro himself had an equally evident erection and, unbuttoning his jacket, displayed a collection of ladies' garters, sewn into the lining as trimmings. He had a whole collection of these feminine, mythological trappings and asked Justine for a small totem of her affection.

Celestina Tropical

I decided to have a look around and noted activity in every corner of the house. The house itself was barely concealed behind an elaborate garden, and walking through its corridors of pallid splendor, my impression was one of a gathering of apparitions, were it not for the gramophone playing in the living room. Two fine hunting dogs were scratching at the runners with powerful paws.

I heard a voice calling to me from somewhere, and as I opened the door I could barely make out a figure stretched out on the bed therein, half hidden by a mosquito netting. The voice was childlike and beckoned me closer. I lifted the mosquito netting and could just delineate the contours of a woman in the darkness. My hand was guided along a thigh of caressively soft skin, as I succumbed to the lingering aroma of femininity.

My hand was led to a moist profusion of curly hair, but neither one of us uttered a sound, save of our own breathing. I was really in a daze, it was quite dark, and her hand was now unbuttoning my trousers. That same hand began to stroke me and I could barely move about in the darkness. Until, suddenly, a bell rang out shrilly and all the lights in the house were automatically turned on. A girl of, at most, twelve years of age was wetting her lips and staring at me. In that land, even puberty was precocious.

Márcio Souza

The Crusades

In Acre, at that moment, no one seemed preoccupied with precocious puberties. On a rubber plantation known as New Jerusalem, owned by Felismino Meira, five men were tied to a treetrunk and tortured to death. The reason: attempted flight after running up heavy debts at the plantation's supply depot. At the same time, in the city of Puerto Alonso, a group of Brazilians were zestfully deposing the Bolivian prefect of police, on behalf of the Acrean people and all Brazilian citizens besides. Few Brazilian citizens, however, actually even knew where Acre was, in 1899.

Lesson in Ideology

FREIRE: *Voilà comme on apprend à tuer les seringueros.*
GALVEZ: *Manaos n'est qu'une ville romantique.*

Ballet Mystique

The downstairs room was now opulently lighted, and a number of footmen were serving the evening meal. Interesting to note: in that city no one seemed to have any face, only imported clothes and *bijouteries*. A circular table had been moved to the middle of the room, and a woman already on in years appeared holding a candelabrum and exhibiting a certain tarnished sensuality. Major Freire explained to me that for several sessions they had been trying, unsuccessfully, to summon Victor Hugo. All that they had managed to cull were a few Indians and some old, black slaves—lowly apparitions who screamed with horror while uttering obscenities. According to Madame Vitrac, the hoary pythoness, there were a great number of inferior spirits in the tropical ether. Justine whispered in my ear, asking to go. It was already late and the street was totally deserted. Since we couldn't find any hansom, we started to walk down Avenida Sete de Setembro.

Feminine Psychology

JUSTINE: *Ils sont très aimables avec les femmes, les brésiliens. . . .*
GALVEZ: *Je suis jaloux!*

Metropolis

Life in Manaus was twice as expensive as in Paris. The Teatro Amazonas, which Sir Henry insisted was the work of extraterrestrials, had actually cost the government coffers more than 400,000 pounds sterling. A lunch at a modest restaurant wouldn't go for less than six dollars. It was there that you had the highest per capita consumption of diamonds in the world. The *nouveaux arrivés* adored breaking records. At the home of Major Freire, an ingot of gold served as a paperweight.

An Adventurer's Repose

I awoke beside Justine, a most appealing *paysage*. Her body turning over in the sheets. The noise of the street impertinently invading the room's semi-shadow. My laziness vanished immediately from my limbs. To be there beside Justine L'Amour was more than just a privilege for anyone who had been marooned on the Rio Amazonas. It was a deserved repose.

My Desire

I had been expecting little more than a few nice nocturnal surprises. After all, the cities of the frontier were at least prodigal with their pleasures. Yet I had already accustomed myself to a taste for the superfluous so ardently cultivated by the lords of latex, not to mention having learned to live with monotony.

Théâtre de Prosper Mérimée

Justine opened her eyes and looked at me with the spirit of the epoch in her stare. She was cultivating the nightlife with serenity. Justine L'Amour had a penchant for being above it all.

Pilgrim's Progress

My noble British scientist friend returned, all enthusiastic, from the upper Rio Negro. The ceremonies of Jurupari had been uninhibited orgies which lasted for days. Sir Henry told me that Manaus was also possessed by the same Dionysian spirit, offering as it did the greatest array of erotic paraphernalia in all of South America. His dreams had become quite turbulent, and now the eminent scientist was allowing himself to indulge in oral practices with his entourage. Sir Henry was sleeping nearly twelve hours a day—the only case of an *aficionado* of nocturnal pollutions I encountered in all my life.

Syncretism

The English presence in Manaus was so strong that there were even a few traditional apparitions. At a certain palazzo, by a wrought-iron bridge, on a particular hour of the night, with the precision of Greenwich time, it was possible to catch a glimpse of the pale specter of a blind woman—her eyes torn out by revenge—or the bloody figure of an earl, in eighteenth-century costume. Sir Henry felt relatively at home in that city.

Mail Bag

João Lúcio wrote me from Paris, where he was taking a cure; nothing serious. France continued agitated by the

Dreyfus case. General Chanoine was attempting to declare a military dictatorship. A right-winger had nearly managed a *coup d'état*, as Europe appeared to be imitating the tropics. Cira was with Alberto, in Vichy. Dona Eudóxia, the pianist, had fled Pará with a Chinese prestidigitator.

A Tale of the Amazonas

I went shopping with Major Freire on a steamship of the Booth Line, docked in the harbor. Freire wanted to pick up a panama hat for himself. He was irritatedly browsing around with his coterie of adolescents, and kept throwing the hats he didn't like into the river. Ninety hats had soared into the Rio Negro when the major finally came across a panama to his liking.

Fountain of Youth

In Manaus, there were three lively streets with boarding-house facilities that included French amenities. Business hours began at four in the afternoon. An encounter with a thirteen-year-old whore alleging virginity might cost you seventy pounds not including refreshments. "Libertad" and her poodle would run you close to "five hundred more, door to door," as in the old infantry round. An entire night of pleasure was set at fifteen hundred pounds. Of course, one had at one's disposal a veritable League of Nations: Muscovites, Arabs, Hungarians, etc. And cooling sugar-cane crushes to prevent inflammations.

Tropical Afternoons

I donned my *sakko* and straightened my "boater." The street was broiling and there was a smell of rotting fruit and sweated horses. Occasional Americans cut across the wide promenades. Mestizos were selling lottery tickets. By the doorways of the taverns, along the Avenida do Palácio, chairs were scattered about like skeletons in a desert. Canvas awnings did little to ward off the sun, and the restaurants themselves seemed deadly still beneath the slowly turning ceiling fans. I sat with Thaumaturgo and began to read a copy of *Le Matin*. My friend Vaez still retained a pronounced Northeastern accent and somehow called to mind Plato's venerable *Republic*. He told me that a colonel from Manaus had outbid the Baron de Roth-schild at an auction. The Portuguese had never managed to implant a civilization there, even on the level of a Rio de Janeiro. Thaumaturgo actually predicted the failure of the Banco da República. The bright light in the restaurant neutralized the dark suits, the red wines, and tinny gramophone. We consumed the same silence that was uselessly spinning the blades on the fans. Sitting beneath that meager breath of air while the streets slowly emptied. Manaus respected only the indolence of midday, its movements diminishing to a reptilian repose, as it finally congealed to a heat that coincided with the meeting of two clock hands. Much later, the sun would relent and allow a skeletal reanimation which would anguish on into the night.

The Inclinations of a Poet

Thaumaturgo Vaez led me to a shop where one presumably bought matches. Two still-youngish-looking, tawny females of an Amazonian cast—short stature, bronzed skin (from sultriness rather than sunshine), ample bodies, and strong legs—proceeded to charge us an exorbitant price for a box of matches.

My Matches

I went into an adjoining room of the shop and noticed an alcove . . . mirrors, two wicker easy chairs, an iron bedstead secluded by a silk curtain. My salesgirl looked to be about seventeen. She sat on the edge of the bed, lifted her skirt, and began to take off her stockings in such a way as to afford me a full view of her scarlet artifice. She got out of the dress with my assistence and we went to bed. I inserted myself effortlessly into her humid interior and she responded with sighs. Her skin was burning. I became quite sweated, slowly pumping with a firm grip on her breasts. I think we put in a fair amount of time at it, and I eventually noticed that there were quite a number of flies in the room.

Pedagogy

The two matchgirls were fruits of the educative effort of Major Freire. They had originally come as maids, from his properties in Juruá. Their interest in the arts of Venus had been awakened as a result of several preliminary excursions into the world of the spirits. Then Freire, reading a book of English pornography, came across the story of the matchgirls who so concerned themselves with putting out men's fires. He gave the young girls lessons and financed the shop. So very Victorian, come now, major. . . .

Picturesque Amazonas

But don't go judging a place by the dissipated life of an adventurer. In my three months of Amazonas, my experience was practically dominated by the pleasures of nocturnal bohemianism. True, there aren't many options in a city of twenty thousand souls, where one egg from a chicken costs three dollars, and even so, there still seems to be plenty of money for omelettes. And the eggs are all imported.

In a city of that kind, it's only natural for bourgeois morality and mercantile love to enter into conflict, with neither one coming out unscathed. Obviously, no man contented himself with family life. Living in the nineteenth century, but still clinging to sixteenth-century obsessions. All of them so divided and rapacious. Major Freire, for instance, was married to a genteel lady who was a granddaughter of the governor. I met this unhappy woman at an official reception. She was lovely, albeit abysmally ill informed. A semi-illiterate, she spent days locked up in her home, embroidering and reading idiotic stories. Yet she didn't know she was unhappy, thinking only that she suffered some chronic infirmity. The major would not allow her to go out unescorted and probably made love to her once a year. The proof? Seven children out of eight years of marriage. . . . And Major Freire, the most famous libertine in all of Manaus. Well, sex obliged money to have more of an imagination.

The Age of Enlightenment

Sir Henry continued to dream of Jurupari and was busy writing a lengthy monograph on his travels. The work was to be entitled *From the Orinoco to the Blue Slipper Café*, and was to relate various aspects of a society dominated by a libidinous extraterrestrial godhead. The space ship of Jurupari, according to a design found on a rock in São Gabriel da Cachoeira, was an immense phallus with an ejaculatory trajectory. Sir Henry invited me to assume an office in his research society. I would receive a handsome stipend and could return with him to London, where we might finally organize the vast amount of materials he had collected from the region. I told him I would have to think about it.

Vade Mecum of Comportment

I guess everyone prevaricates in this city. . . . I read in the *Jornal do Comércio* that the managing director himself of the Teatro Amazonas was caught red-handed conspurcating the carpet of the governor's box with a chorus girl from the Compagnia Giovanni Emanuele. They claimed to be discussing the low birthrate in Paris at the time. Sir Henry saw in this, however, capital proof by which to fix the center of biocosmic powers within the monument. He also confessed to me that no sooner would he penetrate the precincts of the theater than he would get an erection.

Ming Dynasty

Thaumaturgo, who really doesn't miss a trick, took me to meet a Chinese couple, professing to be miracle workers, who practiced acupuncture and removed cataracts with crochet needles. The "oriental" wife was none other than Dona Eudóxia, the pianist, who apparently didn't recognize me and was busy mixing her *l*'s and *r*'s to achieve a convincingly Cantonese accent. Her chopstick of a husband barely measured a meter and a half in height. The two of them were being expelled from the city at the behest of the medical profession; they were curing venereal diseases at noncompetitive rates.

Even Adventurers Sometimes Get Weary

The ills of isolation have infected me. If I fail to see a steamer in the harbor, I am quickly overcome by melancholy and begin to fear the possibility of never escaping this jungle prison again. Yet I can hardly curse the jungle, given the extent to which it brings men together here (even if they fail to appreciate the fact). Hemmed in, the all-powerful indulge in society. Manaus would never have grown into a city were it not for its isolation. I have been giving serious thought to Sir Henry's proposal.

The Eternal Return

Along about that warmish month of May, Joana finally showed up again. The same ruddy blush gently rising to her temples, the nervous hands that still recalled the problematical sister of charity. But gone were the shy exchanges whispered back and forth in that ecclesiastical hold. Joana had come back, but transformed by that milieu of chorus girls from which she was hardly distinguishable. It was still a joy to set eyes upon my companion in ambiguity. Justine was busy admiring the attractive cut of Joana's dress. But the two of us quickly escaped to the street.

Promenade

She was smiling to me like a suburban sweetheart, her straight hair flowing over her shoulders. A big hat with a floppy brim, white like the fitted bodice that so elegantly accentuated her form. There was quite a bit of mud on the streets, plowed up by the wheels of the carriages. The sidewalks seemed to be coated with an aluminous film. I'd slept rather poorly and my hair wasn't combed. Joana noticed how tired I was and offered to buy me some fried chips with mustard. She was teaching in a public school but thinking of applying for a post somewhere in the interior of the state. I asked her if it wasn't enough to live in Manaus, and Joana answered that she would feel more useful teaching in the interior.

Ideological Minuet

What I am about to say has nothing to do with my conversation with Joana. We climbed the Avenida do Palácio and walked along the sidewalk fronting the Hall of Justice, a building in the classical style, but of reduced proportions. My attention was awakened by the statue of Justice, personified to the taste of the Directory and sheltered in the pediment of the building itself. Only she wasn't blindfolded, and seemed to have her eyes wide open. The merchants of latex knew that Justice did not amount to more than a poetic license of the eighteenth century. Even the law had to watch its step in the Amazonas.

Orphans of the Storm

Joana was only twenty, but already felt uneasy in the face of the rapid transformation of Manaus. When she was still a little child, the streets had no pavement, and most of the houses were built of wood and lacked electricity, water, or sewage. A trip to Belém invariably took three months. Joana's father had arrived there in 1865, from the state of Maranhão, only to find a sad little hamlet with a few streets, too much mud, and five thousand souls huddled together. By the time Joana was fifteen and her father held a reception for two hundred guests, the city numbered twenty thousand.

Calvary Revisited

Joana must have been one of those adolescents burdened by sensitivity. Easily swayed, she had quickly surrendered herself to the protectiveness of the Catholic Church, to which she planned to consecrate her life. She confessed to me that religion was the only strong and changeless world she felt she could trust in. Her temperament also required a great deal of discipline. Walking next to me, she seemed wonderful, though still surprised with the growing changes within herself. I recognized a young girl's furtive escape and sudden discovery of the world around her. From the instant I saw her, I knew it to be one of those rare moments in life when a person becomes free. And it was only a few more days before she took off her clothes to show me her new self in what must have amounted to a deliberate ceremony. We were so alone that I cannot even consider myself an accomplice.

Advertisement

On the wall, a poster: miraculous cures for malaria, insomnia, hookworm, neurasthenia, fevers, tremors, itches, venereal diseases—try Giffoni Elixir, Milan. Twenty Italian press operators, from Fênix Typography, Inc., were also out on strike and busy distributing anarchistic manifestoes.

Motives for an Adventurer

Joana went about enthusiastic with her new life, and we traded opinions on Acre. It was to Acre that Joana intended to go, and so the fate of that paradise of endemic tropical diseases once again entered my life with those conversations we had together. And Joana had no intention of relying upon the comfortable realm of favor. She was working directly with political activists, preparing herself to one day experience the thralls of a veritable revolution. To teach in the Territory of Acre was a revolutionary act worthy of her missionary soul.

Joana was also aware of what an American presence would represent in the territory. Such awareness amounted to a healthy instinct for self-preservation. . . . Threats had already made it quite evident that no manifest destiny was going to assure the eternity of the latex colonels once the Americans got a grip on Acre. And Joana told me that the government of Amazonas, cognizant of the danger, had placed at the disposal of interested parties a veritable fortune. All that was needed now was a leader to organize the movement and take on the responsibility of involvement in a serious international affair.

Joana had already learned of my adversity in Belém— for Acre's sake—and considered me to be in the ambiguous profession of adventurer. . . . Therefore, quite capable of ignoring danger and drawing about a charismatic self the aspirations of the merchants of latex. She felt certain that my destiny was inextricably linked to Acre, even if at that moment I shared none of her caprice. Toward evening, when the Southern Cross was already sparkling in the heavens, she invited me to participate in an illustrious gathering, to take place there at the Hotel Cassina, of some of the notables in the movement. An invitation which sounded so familiar to me that I couldn't imagine refusing.

In the Name of Science

When I next had dinner with Sir Henry, Justine—who had by now become a frequent guest aboard the bark of science—told me that our friend had brought back some curios from his long trip up the Rio Negro. After dinner, Sir Henry invited me to come have a tour of the cabin where the precious relics were being guarded. And precious relics they were, since my dear Dr. Lust was housing— in jars of formaldehyde—close to twenty samples of masculine genitalia, garnered from Indians of the Rio Vaupés.

All in a Night's Work

When he was trying to enter into contact with the Tariana Indians, Sir Henry had suffered an ambush and lost a grip on his nerves. He fired pell-mell and struck down two natives. They were handsome young warriors, and left the scientist feeling quite consternated, since he was a man of peace. The dead Indians were a little over a meter and a half tall and, upon closer examination of the bodies, Sir Henry's consternation turned to amazement. The so-called private parts of those two strapping savages were so inordinately developed that they would have humiliated any mortal. With tremulous hands, the good doctor amputated the two genitalia and guarded them in flasks of wine spirits. "We were immediately struck by the disproportional configuration of those instruments," Sir Henry grunted to me between swallows of white wine, "and took it to be a potent manifestation of powers outside the scope of everyday reality. We knew of the flutes of Jurupari, of course, and now these virile sexual organs were there to amply confirm the libidinous origins of that extraterrestrial intervention." Sir Henry lifted one of the flasks, where a phallus, albeit a little shrunken, floated in the liquid with its imposing thirty-three centimeters of extension. "In hopes of further corroborating our findings, we offered to scouts accompanying our expedition a bounty of thirty pounds for an example in perfect physical condition. We received all that you see here, and I cannot fault the diligence with which those rustic foragers plied their understanding of the scientific method."

Contretemps

Sir Henry complained that he was being detained, there in Manaus, precisely because of this array of precious specimens. The Amazonas customs had refused to release his cargo and had requested further instructions from the federal capital. The customs officers tended to view his collection as an encroachment upon the virility of the nation. In that same week, however, a letter from the Minister of Finance would free the collection as objects for personal use—a courtesy on the part of the federal authorities to foster the progress of humanity.

Márcio Souza

Descartes

Eyeing those flasks carefully packed in cardboard boxes full of straw, I let my port wine wash slowly down my throat. I placed the crystal glass back on the table and saw my future with Sir Henry. . . . No, I had no intention of spending the rest of my life looking for vestiges of space-men among Savages. Or comparing those genitals that seemed to so attract the curiosity of Justine L'Amour. Sir Henry may have represented an option for a more solvent financial situation, but I could never give him serious consideration. True, I was approaching poverty, and at the moment, very distant from the axis of power wielded in the province. I had totally avoided becoming involved with the elite there, and my only real friend in the territory —the poet Thaumaturgo—was a *bon vivant* who brought me animated weekends and spirited conversation. Sir Henry, however, had taught me that the Teatro Amazonas was architecturally too intricate to allow one a quick, clean getaway . . . even in a *feuilleton*.

Guide Michelin to Manaus

The Hotel Cassina was not the ideal location to spend a quiet holiday. According to its publicity, it was the busiest hotel in all of Christendom, an evident exaggeration which nevertheless gained a certain credence with all the coming and going in the corridors. It was definitely not a hotel for the proverbial well-deserved rest; its sweaty guests were there to assuage other needs.

Yet on that particular afternoon, the hotel restaurant had more the look of a military mess hall than a setting for out-of-the-ordinary nocturnal diversions. As incredibly dirty and totally disordered as the restaurant was by morning, a squad of diligent domestics would daily arrive on the scene, like a precisely timed rescue operation, and have everything back in order before lunch. True, it wasn't a posh restaurant, but the decor had its good points once

119

you placed it in the proper context. Wallpaper with oriental designs, curtains of green silk, and ornate wall sconces of electrical lighting garishly mounted over the former gas outlets. Round tables and flimsy chairs . . . and to the left of anyone climbing the stairs (the restaurant was located on the mezzanine), a track of footlights covered in red velvet.

On that particular afternoon, then, the restaurant was suitably clean but noticeably empty, with its windows shut and a high humidity dominating the penumbra. And upon entering I discovered five tables pushed together into the middle of the dining room, as if to accommodate some special occasion. One of the figures conversing in the dim light suddenly directed a familiar voice to me. It was Joana, who presented me to everyone; and I met the Governor of Amazonas himself, the legendary Colonel Ramalho Júnior, a man of extraordinary polish, who was accustomed to presenting "maestros" with batons of solid gold, and strings of real pearls to chorus girls.

A Sense of Destiny

Present at that reunion—besides Joana and the governor —were my friend Vaez, Major Freire, Congressman Mesquita, Colonel Epaminondas Valle, and the lawyer (not to mention latex merchant and plantation owner) Júlio Araújo. In Manaus, the presence of so many notables, gathered together for an afternoon at the Hotel Cassina, would have surprised no one. And it was the type of orgy in which Joana felt unconstrained about her own participation. The Hotel Cassina is, after all, but a short distance —a few meters—from the Government Palace.

Structural Monoculture

I am not going to bore the reader with the subject of that reunion. I was hardly listening with any great conviction myself to that stimulating series of arguments. It was useless to apply any established rules of understanding to the world of commercial extraction. Neither Aristotle nor Machiavelli . . . In fact, all my science—derived from a temperate climate—was incapacitated by the 30° Celsius of an Amazonian afternoon. And the vaudevillian ladder of life was no respecter of expectations. . . . Yet they looked to me, full of curiosity, as even my silence seemed to cut through their arguments. They were eager, all right, enraptured with the mystery of the adventurer they saw in me, observing me as if I were capable of some magical attitude. For my part, I found the whole thing tedious. And I looked upon Joana with a certain pity. Until the governor offered to strike a favorable balance: fifty thousand pounds (sterling). And so a simple *malentendu*, originating in an attic in Pará and leading to fisticuffs at the premiere of an opera, continued to challenge me like a card game among incompetents. But to gamble with incompetents, even when the prize is fifty thousand pounds, is still rather tedious. At the moment, Attorney Araújo, Esq., was delivering a formidably eloquent discourse on the sacrifices of myriad Northeasterners who had struggled so ably to build Acre, when I unexpectedly interrupted to say I would accept. Colonel Ramalho Júnior applauded and proceeded to order some champagne.

Acrean Obligations

For the sum of fifty thousand pounds, I was obliged to liberate Acre from Bolivian domination, declaring the territory free and independent. Then I was to form a government which would attempt to gain international recognition. Once all this should be accomplished, my government was to solicit annexation by Brazil. My nationality would allay any suspicion of the latter's involvement. As to form of government, to them it was immaterial.

Plato's Republic

I first thought of a dictatorship, since every man dreams of satisfying an infantile inclination to command without limits. I then considered Hobbes' State, but saw it would require a stage of development far too advanced for the tropics. Turning to a utopia (*à la* Sir Thomas More), I immediately realized that it would not be interpreted as a form of government at all. So I decided in favor of a monarchy: full of pomp, *esprit de corps*, and local color— like a national holiday.

Revolutionary Toast

The waiters served champagne, and Colonel Ramalho Júnior proposed a toast to an independent Acre. I looked over at Joana, and she had the solemn air of someone who was actually witnessing the birth of a nation. This game of myopic partners did not cease to have its moments of solemnity. Which lent life a certain charm, I suppose. . . .

Richard Coeur de "Latex"!

Sir Henry offered me some advice about monarchies. I should avoid Bonapartism and any parliaments with the power of veto. He sorely lamented the lack of a queen mother, so necessary to young nations. And as soon as my country had a capital, Sir Henry would come to inaugurate a branch of his Metaphysical Society. A form of international recognition.

Sir Henry was irritable of late, and would unfortunately involve himself in a lamentable incident some two hours after our meeting together. At the High-Life Saloon, in full view of everyone, challenging the cries of "Impostor," he leveled two shots at Colonel Eduardo Ribeiro, which luckily struck no one. Then once the crowd had recovered from their amazement and come out from various hiding places, they caught sight once more of the good doctor, crossing the street with his pants unbuttoned and his private parts on public display. He was quickly arrested and then later freed on direct orders from the governor. According to several witnesses, Sir Henry could compete on an equal footing, so to speak, with his entire collection of indigenous genitalia. Reason enough to make me understand the tireless devotion to science of Justine L'Amour, that insatiable *femme de la France*.

Agenda

—Set up a Revolutionary Committee to prepare the various stages of the movement.
—Set up an Intelligence Network to collect
data on the Bolivian presence in Acre.
—Set up an office for recruiting volunteers.
—Set up an office to administer the commissariat and munitions.
—Rent a campground for the military training
of raw recruits.

Maneuvers

May 1899. One month is not exactly time enough to
prepare oneself for a revolution. But who is ready to
affirm that any amount of time is enough to prepare a
revolution? I named Marthe, Concetta, and Marie to run
our Intelligence Network. Thaumaturgo Vaez offered the
grounds of his house, on the outskirts of town, for
military training and maneuvers.

Coded Message I

Stationed in Acre, the Bolivians had but one detachment of militia—no more than thirty men—armed with
rifles, which offered more intimidation than any real threat
of danger. (Information gathered by Concetta, at an intimate moment with the Bolivian vice-consul, Loyasa.)
Thirty Indian recruits, shoeless and toothless, who seemed
to outshine everyone only at the evening brawls over in
Puerto Alonso's prostitution district. (Information gathered by Marthe, in the private office of the Bolivian
merchant Perez de Amayo, between pledges of love.)

Henry the Eighth

Sir Henry left Amazonas on the S.S. *Liverpool*. His
oneiric sessions with Jurupari were almost daily and highly

erotic. Cosmic orgies in a setting of electricity and primitivism. During one dream alone, the mythic figure deflowered two hundred virgins, and Sir Henry awoke exhausted.

Coded Message II

The caliber of Bolivian weapons was a joke, and they were always jamming in the heat of battle. (Information gathered by Marie, in fieldwork carried out with the Bolivian merchant Caballar; age 70, height 1.7 meters, weight 60 kilos.)

What Is to Be Done?

We were encouraged by the state of the enemy troops, and the animation in Manaus appeared to guarantee the immediate success of our plans. I tried to partake of the reigning optimism, even if I still found the boundless confidence everybody seemed to place in me inexplicable. I was being treated like a shrewd old *caudillo* and veteran of an invincible store of military expertise. I armed myself with apparent humility before that ardent if uneven force, recruited by Vaez from among the more bohemian elements of the Hotel Cassina. Observing those shock troops of depraved Romeo's, lured to Thaumaturgo's farm by promises of ale, my revolution offered me no great hopes—even against such a wretched band of enemies as I was apparently to face. But the pounds sterling had seduced me, nonetheless. So I was arranging everything in such a manner that it would present no greater risk to my person than an uncomfortable sea voyage. I was going to carry out a few manifestations in Puerto Alonso, in front of a mass of country yokels. I would turn my charade of a revolution into an impeccable performance. And to tell the whole truth, my Amazonian period had not been lacking in opportunities for genuine practical experience. I could already consider myself a quasi-specialist in colonial *faits-divers*, a position no decent Spaniard would ever dispense with without first pushing his advantage to the utmost.

Márcio Souza

Environmental Statistics

The mean temperature in Acre is 28° Celsius, with an average humidity of around 70%. Its territory covers 72,580 square miles. My kingdom was twice the size of Portugal.

A Morning of Hot Sun and Cold Beer

When I arrived at Vaez's farm (a lovely lawn with leafy avocado and cashew trees, let me say in passing), I was not to be welcomed with the customary honors—or even an austere military salute worthy of a crack revolutionary brigade—but by a hearty toast of foamy ale. My expeditionary force, already a little groggy from the continuous exercise of emptying tankards of ale, cheered raucously. The prevailing good humor (though in the face of certain grim possibilities) was a sign that my revolution would never be defeated for lack of enthusiasm. And the poet Vaez, proud of his intoxicated revolutionaries—who were battling like Hussars, there's no denying it, against the forces of gravity—came to brief me on the general aptitudes of each of his volunteers. They were eternal students, chronic vagabonds, unpublished poets, black sheep from august families, pettifogging attorneys; confederates all, by virtue of the incurable insomnia that obliged them to burn the candle at both ends, the year round together.

Ballistics

If my troops were obliged to use firearms, they wouldn't know which end of the rifle to point at the enemy. An irrelevant problem for men who were ever alert to detect a false Scotch whisky or a vintage wine. Only Fate herself knew how useful such alcoholic aptitudes would prove to be in the heat of battle.

General Headquarters

GALVEZ: We just might conquer the world, if we don't die of cirrhosis of the liver first.

VAEZ: They're the best we've got. . . .

GALVEZ: Any problems?

VAEZ: One casualty. Zequinha Farias, our piano player, passed away yesterday at Misericordia Hospital.

GALVEZ: *Causa mortis?*

VAEZ: Syphilis.

GALVEZ: Order the flag at half mast. . . .

Official Communiqué I

FROM: Commandant Galvez
TO: Chief Commissary Officer
Dear Sir: I have decided to order a readjustment in our purchase schedule. Please be so good as to lower the number of cases of munitions by four, and thereby increase the wine allotment by two cases and the beer by twenty dozen.

> Revolutionary Greetings,
> Long Live Independent Acre!
> Galvez, Commander-in-Chief

Official Communiqué II

FROM: Chief Commissary Officer
TO: Commandant Galvez
Dear Sir: As per your instructions, the readjustment is already underway. We also take the liberty of suggesting that the Commandant likewise authorize the purchase of eight cases of White Horse, currently on sale at the Guerra Grocery. An incredible steal!

> Revolutionary Greetings,
> Long Live Independent Acre!
> José Fernando, Chief Officer

Official Communiqué III

FROM: Commandant Galvez
TO: Chief Commissary Officer
Dear Sir: Welcome suggestion; White Horse
is a fine whisky and the price is right. We have
also been informed that our Acrean regiments
smell rather bad. For this reason, and in the
interests of the prestige of the revolution itself,
we authorize the purchase of two barrels of
Lublin toilet water. A sweet-smelling people
are a civilized people.

> Revolutionary Greetings,
> Long Live Independent Acre!
> Galvez, Commander-in-Chief

The Marvels of Monoculture

I was asleep in my room at the Hotel Cassina when
Blangis came in to awaken me with the news that an international assemblage had just taken up quarters in the same
hotel. The Bolivians, who numbered five in all, came
accompanied by an equal number of Brazilian officials
from the Ministry of Foreign Relations. Luiz Trucco and
Michael Kennedy had also come along as observers. All
were en route to Puerto Alonso, where they would decide
once and for all the fate of Acre.

The dignitaries, Brazilian as well as Bolivian, were elderly statesmen of vast experience, full of shrewd talk
and studied gestures. They had arrived on a modern,
Italian-built packet ship—carrying almost no baggage—
and were being ceremoniously led about by the famous
cane of old Trucco. The Bolivian consul, however, wearing
a white *sakko* in the blazing sun, refused to participate
in the informality of the remaining dignitaries. I suspect
that he was quite furious with the reception on the part
of the Amazonas government, which had only dispatched
a subordinate official from the Ministry of Justice to welcome them. (The official indifference of the state of Amazonas was Colonel Ramalho Júnior's way of manifesting his

personal displeasure, and Trucco began to guard himself warily against attack.)

They had been driven, for some reason, to the Hotel Cassina, where no reservations had been made for them. Accommodated there, our dignitaries were at the moment taking their leisure (a lovely *art-nouveau* expression) in bentwoods out on the verandah, blissfully indifferent to the commotion of the city.

I was hoping that the group would prefer the Grand Hotel—opposite the Magazin Louvre—recently inaugurated and with a reputation for the utmost tranquillity. Agents of the Amazonas government had anticipated Trucco and Kennedy's arrival in Manaus, accompanying a team of demarcation. They had accordingly advised me and even planted a few members of the police among the staff of the Grand Hotel itself, where the governor had troubled to reserve rooms for their stay. After all, that was the more appropriate environment for those who temper their public lives with moderation. In short, an ideal location for a notable assemblage such as theirs.

Even today I cannot adequately account for their having so suddenly changed their minds and installed themselves in the frivolous Hotel Cassina. The government paper *Comércio do Amazonas*, publicizing the fact, managed to float a few suspicions as to the morality of the dignitaries in question, which left Trucco even more irritated.

Théâtre de Beaumarchais I

While the assemblage was seated out on the verandah, I decided a personal investigation was in order. I first dispatched my agents Marthe, Marie, and Concetta to try to obtain information from the primary sources. Justine L'Amour decided to work on a voluntary basis, accompanying my agents out to the hotel verandah, much to the delight of the visiting dignitaries. I entered the room where Luiz Trucco was quartered and stole a collection of maps. In Kennedy's room I found absolutely nothing; it was untouched, without even sheets or blanket left on the bed.

Cartography

The maps Trucco had were worthless and could be picked up in any stationery store.

Théâtre de Beaumarchais II

Out on the porch, meantime, Justine L'Amour was elaborating to listeners her extensive martyrdom. Michael Kennedy grew suddenly interested when it came to the effects of yellow fever, which had decimated the Compagnie Opératique de la France and led to its demise. Trucco was also visibly moved by the misfortunes of the actress. My agents were certainly making progress, but my problem was that I had to move out of the hotel, immediately, yet without arousing suspicion. I would take up quarters at Vaez's house, where I could oversee all operations in tight security. My exodus from the hotel, however, was a masterpiece of pantomime, ably assisted by the "maestro" Blangis himself.

Psychological Warfare

The conversation suddenly palled when a cadaver, draped in a sheet, lying on a stretcher, born along by two attendants from Misericordia Hospital, exited through the front door of the Hotel Cassina. All rose and took off their hats, in a last salute to the fallen guest. Following the stretcher and carefully keeping an eye on the two porters who were lugging out the baggage of the deceased walked an inconsolable Blangis. Seeing that the body was so heavy, Trucco himself assisted the attendants in sliding the corpse into the waiting ambulance. Meanwhile, Blangis was wistfully relating to the American that the deceased had been a victim of chronic beriberi. He had trembled for years, always laughing, always amusing himself and his friends, and had seemed to have strength enough to continue cheerfully trembling for quite a few more years yet. Kennedy, however, only wanted to know where the victim had contracted the disease in the first place. Blangis answered that he was a merchant, from Acre, where the affliction was endemic. Kennedy turned visibly pale.

Pride and Prejudice

Michael Kennedy suffered from an irrational fear of contracting one of those terrible tropical infirmities. A fear that reached the exaggerated proportions of his totally isolating himself, even in Belém. And his aloofness made him a target of indecent gossip and malicious insinuations. If he finally put in a brief appearance at a reception, he wouldn't touch the food or wine; and whenever he left Belém he was accompanied by his black majordomo, who would personally prepare his meals. All of his articles of consumption were sent to him from the United States, including the very water with which he took his bath. No one was permitted to enter his room, where everything was painstakingly disinfected with alcohol. Kennedy did not like to shake anybody's hand; he noticed something corruptive about the tropics, amply confirmed by the waves of poverty-stricken emigrants from the Northeast, not to mention the emaciated features and Indian complexion of a more indigenous population.

Family Life

Michael Kennedy remained in Brazil only to please his mother, a poor widow from early on. Mr. Kennedy had died in Texas while trying to build a cattle empire. He had fallen, riddled with bullets, during an unsuccessful assault on a Mexican train. Mrs. Kennedy, a woman of tough moral fiber, became a dressmaker in Chicago, sacrificing herself in order to keep her young Michael at Harvard, where he would graduate as a lawyer and go on to become an official in the State Department. Mrs. Ken-

nedy was likewise frightened to death of infirmities arising
from those pestilential regions south of the Rio Grande;
after all, she had already seen her own husband devastated
by malaria, contracted in Guatemala, where he had gone
to manage the affairs of the Caribbean Fruit Company,
Ltd. Michael was only twelve when his father was confined to a hospital bed, delirious from fever and trembling
with cold.

Latin Perspicacity

Trucco observed when Michael Kennedy (his hands
tremulous, his face perspiring) retreated to a corner, only
to end up rocking pensively back and forth in an easy
chair. He knew well enough about the American's peculiar-
ities, but he liked Michael, nonetheless; the way one likes
a foolish, rich, and powerful little boy. Trucco was only
irritated when his friend would refuse his repeated invita-
tions to dine with him (with Trucco, that is) at his own
home. After all, in all his existence as a tropical being,
Trucco had never contracted even the slightest chill, dis-
counting the chicken pox at nine and gonorrhea (not worth
mentioning) at seventeen.

Grand Guignol

The ambulance took the road to Cachoeirinha, bouncing over the railroad tracks. I came back to life with
cackles of laughter, and the jostling in the ambulance transformed my laughter into convulsions. The two stretcher
bearers crossed themselves and stopped to check what was
going on back there. When they opened up the rear, they
found me quite resurrected, sitting on the stretcher. Their
fear was so outspoken that I had to pay quite a tidy sum
to shut their mouths. I arrived at Vaez's house sitting up
in the carriage box and driving the horses myself, given
that the two attendants still eyed me mistrustfully, as much
from the tip as from shock.

Charge of the Light Brigade

To the sound of a ragtime beat, blaring from a gramophone in the shade of an avocado tree, Vaez was drilling my troops.

Special Communiqué

FROM: Commandant Galvez
TO: Chief Commissary Officer
Dear Sir: We wish to communicate that the General Staff, at a meeting of CFG.H5467 and after due deliberation, has decided to condemn the recent purchases of several cases of Heinekker beer, a Dutch brand exhibiting a rather suspect taste. The General Staff, having tested several brands, recommends the following: Munich, São Gonçalo, and Pérola. And finally, the General Staff has seen fit to increase the allotment of champagne, and to add one case of *jerez* for the exclusive use of the Commandant.

Revolutionary Greetings,
Long Live Independent Acre!
Galvez, Commander-in-Chief

Dispatch

The Commander-in-Chief of the Acrean Revolution, utilizing his legal prerogatives, hereby resolves:

1) To authorize the rank of Brigadier General for citizen Thaumaturgo Vaez, with a monthly stipend of $400.
2) To authorize the rank of Colonel for citizen François Blangis, with a monthly stipend of $300.
3) To authorize the rank of Major for citizen José Fernando, with a monthly stipend of $200.
4) To draft for active service in the Revo-

Márcio Souza

lutionary Army—as intelligence officers—citizens Marthe Renoud, Concetta Cezari, Marie Anelli, and Justine L'Amour, with a monthly stipend of $160 plus clothing and expenses.

Long Live the Revolution!
Long Live Independent Acre!
Commander-in-Chief of the Acrean Revolution

Cordial Salute

The following signatories, activists in the Acrean Revolution and members of the Revolutionary Army, in general assembly and by unanimous acclamation, have voted to proclaim Commandant Luiz Galvez Rodrigues de Aria FIELD MARSHAL and LEADER, and do hereby entreat him to accede to the same.

Long Live the Revolution!
Long Live Independent Acre!
Thirty-six signatures follow:

Act of Gratitude

ORDER OF THE DAY
My Comrades: Your attitude has touched me deeply, and shown me how lofty an ideal holds sway in our sublime struggle. I consider your plea an order, my faithful comrades, and but one more proof of the kind of courage that will surely be demonstrated when the hour for sacrifice is at hand. In recognition of the homage you have seen fit to render me, despite my unworthiness, as Commander-in-Chief, Field Marshal, and Leader, I thought it only appropriate to double your salaries and grant everyone three days' leave.

Long Live the Revolution!
Long Live Independent Acre!
Luiz Galvez Rodrigues de Aria,
Field Marshal

133

Casualties

FROM: Chief Medic
TO: Field Marshal Aria
Sir: It behooves me to communicate the demise of Private Jesuíno da Consolação, victim of a severe abdominal blow, striking the *linea alba umbilicus*, severing the *intestinum tenue*, and provoking fatal hemorrhaging. Instrument of the attack: knife. Locality: the Volga Rooming House.

> Long Live the Revolution!
> Long Live Independent Acre!
> Dr. Amarante Nobre de Castro

The Field Doctor

Dr. Nobre, the medic whom Vaez had recruited for my revolution . . . thirty years of practice behind him, he would cure malaria with roots and was the most famous maker of angels in Manaus. He also knew a secret cure for hangovers. . . .

The Pillars of History

Governor Ramalho Júnior offered me a touching homage, on the day prior to our embarking for Acre. During a private dinner at the Government Palace, he asked me what personal desire I still wished to see realized. I answered him that I would one day like to own the house that had once belonged to my father, in Cádiz, and that was presently in the hands of a Jesuit. Ramalho ordered the house repurchased and offered it to me as a present.

Adventures Along the Solimões

The governor had also chartered a small river steamer, the *Esperança,* and placed it at the disposal of Trucco's dignitaries, who immediately read in this a belated sign of civility. The governor had failed to grant either Trucco or Kennedy an audience and also concealed his true reasons for suddenly offering them the transport. For aboard the *Esperança*, shielded by Les Comediens Tropicals and the alcoholics of Thaumaturgo Vaez, I was proceeding in my role of defunct Acrean latex merchant. The coffin of cedar wood, isolated in a cabin, was actually the only detail which had displeased the captain of the steamboat, who nevertheless finally permitted it to be brought on board— hoisted by the unsteady hands of still unsteadier gentlemen—after a great deal of bickering and an additional $200 in freightage.

The irritation of the captain had gained an ally in Kennedy, who, preoccupied with the *causa mortis*, tried to have the coffin detained. But the governor had already warned Luiz Trucco of the matter, alleging the deceased to have been a childhood friend to whom he owed many favors. It was with a great deal of effort, therefore, that Trucco managed to prevent Kennedy from simply returning to Belém. The American had planted himself squarely in the middle of the gangplank, while I was scared to death my recruits might somehow drop me in the water. And Trucco, fed up with the sanitary obsessions of Kennedy, ardently prayed that the next American consul be less of a hypochondriac.

Revolutionary Transport

The S.S. *Esperança*, a 150-footer, was one of those river gypsies without any fixed route: paint worn, crew uncertain, and no clear-cut distinction between first and third class. With almost no hulk below the waterline, she could navigate into any tiny inlet, even at low tide, just as long as the shipment of cashews or rubber adequately compensated her efforts. Soares, the captain, took great pride in never once having gone aground. He was a master of the quick maneuver, bounding out of his cabin whenever the going got rough. . . . The huge wheel at the stern paddled noisily, as we abandoned Manaus on that cold night in June. The steamer's chartered destination was Puerto

Alonso, capital of the Territory of Acre. Her passengers, all illustrious, included several French ladies, one American gentleman (nervous, peculiar, never left his cabin; afraid of malaria), and an embalmed cadaver (to be lowered into its grave on Acrean soil). In the cargo section: animals for slaughter, costumes for the French troupe, lots of liquor. The voyage seemed calm, and Soares was beaming. He had been selected by the governor himself, who had sent an emissary to contract his vessel, over at the Gull's Beak Café, thus adding to his already considerable prestige. For he was one of the few captains who actually knew how to navigate the waters of the Rio Acre, still *aqua incognita*.

Logbook

The voyage began to seem more agreeable once the girls, dressed in showy clothes and led by Justine, went up on the deck of the *Esperança*. Trucco was so absorbed in attending to the American that at first he didn't actually see that the French *mesdames* were on board. He had merely noticed the figure of Justine, in her green silk dress, ascending the stairway up to first class and wondered who was mistress of so lovely a body. He assumed that she must be the widow to the defunct who was provoking so much trepidation in the American. And if Michael did not wish to be infected, that was his business, for Trucco himself was quite willing to risk a case of beriberi if it meant he would get to console the gorgeous widow during those long weeks of mourning until they would dock at Puerto Alonso.

Of Art and Progress

My coffin was suffocating, and I can safely say that those were the worst moments of the entire Revolution, as far as I was concerned. I barely managed to survive the heat, not to mention the beating I took as I was hauled into the cabin. I jumped out of the box, my clothes dripping with sweat, and saw the lights of Manaus receding into the distance. Hours later, we picked up the Rio Solimões, whose waters had begun to recede after a majestic flood tide. Unhappily, my voyage would be restricted for tactical reasons to that bunkless cabin with only one wicker chair.

Trucco finally discovered the French ladies during dinner, and reached the happy conclusion that there existed no sad widows on board. All were ladies who ran no risks of widowhood—even a certain Joana, the new school mistress for Puerto Alonso. A rather timid girl, yet so irritable that Trucco judged her, on the contrary, in urgent need of a man. But it wasn't a male Joana was in need of; she was beginning to be irritated with the crawling pace of the Revolution. She began to come lock herself in my cabin at every opportunity, pressing me with political considerations that had the effect of leaving me also irritated, and in no mood to offer her any gentle understanding.

Seeing the French girls prattling on deck, Trucco unclouded. After all, if any *artistes*, even from a troupe of crazy dreamers, were disposed to offer their entertainments in Acre, it was a sign that some progress was afoot in those lands, until quite recently populated only by bloodthirsty mosquitoes.

Concerning Manners at Table

Everything was truly for the best, as good old Professor Pangloss used to say. Vaez turned out to be the journalist assigned by the *Jornal do Comércio* to cover the trip. As for myself, I was behaving more like a prisoner than a cadaver. My cabin was an oven, barely made endurable by the occasional presence of Justine. As for Joana, she had become some asexual figure whose only concern was politics. Yet no one would suspect that there were revolutionaries traveling aboard. Only one detail might have given us away. Every day an extra plate of food was consumed, which led the captain to suspect a stowaway. But the trip was chartered and nothing was done to clear up the mystery. I was frankly fed up, though, with daily fish chowders of tucunaré, and preferred to amuse myself by counting the money hidden in my cedar coffin. The American mimicked me by never leaving his cabin, though he of course was administered to by his black manservant.

Concerning Manners on Deck

Justine L'Amour did not hide her happiness. She confessed to me that she had high expectations for Acre. If in Manaus, merely through my own contacts, I had managed to accumulate so much money, what *couldn't* she expect of a country where she would become the *prima donna laureata*! Justine was fascinated by power. She would, with her companions, improvise charming musical numbers and cater to the daily whims of the dignitaries. In fact the liberalism of the French ladies, placed as if by chance aboard the same steamer, was the only datum by which Trucco might have computed the political sagacity of the governor of Amazonas. But he couldn't complain, for there was no inconvenience to the happy diversions on deck and in the cabins. A continent or debauched bureaucrat would hardly make a difference at the final hour of decision. Trucco himself spent the days reading a book of Anatole France, keeping an eye on things, and approving with an occasional paternal smile the enthusiasm of the dignitaries. As he leafed through the book, he would read scattered pages, and even came to believe that his initial fears had been unfounded. At such moments he would irritatedly remember Kennedy isolated in his berth, with his bottles of mineral water, canned food, and nauseating preserves.

Concerning Manners in the Berths

Thaumaturgo helped me through that period of trial, organizing animated games of cards which went on until morning. The *Esperança* navigated handsomely up the great river. And in the cabins the activity was no less exciting. There were peals of laughter, the flirtation of French ladies, and Captain Soares took his meals at a table with Trucco, Justine, Vaez, and Blangis. Soares had discovered in Blangis the ideal listener for his own adventures in the Amazon, always suitably spiced with a bit of imagination. Blangis accepted it all with the utmost candor, and even considered Soares a sort of forgotten folk hero.

Márcio Souza

Smiles of a Cold and Windy Morning

In the early-morning hours, as the day was about to begin and life on deck was restricted to the occasional comings and goings of the crew, Kennedy would come out of his cabin, accompanied by his man. He would stroll back and forth in the dwindling darkness and dream of the moment when he would finally return to Belém and resign from the service. He was going back to Chicago and to his house in the suburbs, with its azaleas and no malaria. He would ask for the hand of Constance Benedict, his childhood sweetheart, who was now thirty-two and still waiting. Michael knew that Constance would very likely wait for him all her life, but he wasn't prepared to exact that much of a sacrifice from her. And he would likewise pay a visit to Belle Rose, that spirited woman of the world, who fed him bonbons and spoke so freely of Abilene and its dusty gunslingers, riding roughshod and reeking of cowshit. This when he was back in high school, before Harvard. But Belle Rose would still be there . . . she had to be!

Sexual Life Beyond the Equator

Michael Kennedy was burning with nostalgia and plans for the future when he noticed a light on in the cabin of the deceased. With no greater interest than a slightly morbid curiosity, he walked over to the cabin and took a look through the slats in the shutters. Only to observe a most horrifying scene: Justine, naked, squatting on the pelvis of the corpse in an unmistakable proof that the French go too far in perversity! A Latin opprobrium, no doubt. . . . He had even come across sonnets in the newspapers of Belém which evoked intercourse with cadavers and spoke of ecstasies *d'outre tombe*. Michael backed away appalled by the vision of the splendid figure of Justine, feasting on the fruits of a dead man in a lascivious state of *rigor mortis*. From then on, Kennedy spent the rest of his terrible days believing himself victim of a delirium . . . of some little-known symptom of an even rarer tropical malaise. Now, whenever Justine went by his cabin, Michael was overcome by an impulse to confirm his terrible doubt. He ministered to himself doses of quinine and tried to blot out the macabre vision of the beautiful chorus girl astraddle a mummified corpse, armed with who knows what instruments of passion. And he avoided further morning walks.

Sweat, Rain, and Sultriness

Twenty-eighth of June. Our voyage is almost at an end and Trucco still hasn't finished his book of Anatole France. Blangis has ended up terribly impressed with one adventure of Captain Soares in particular, which apparently included a tribe of Indians that collected heads, in Acre. We had managed to drink eight cases of Scotch whisky. The nineteenth century is draining itself to the last drop, much to my sadness.

Versailles Lost in the Jungle

It was raining heavily. The rafters in the dockside warehouse of the Versailles Plantation shook wet and slippery in the gusty wind, keeping chorus with the clanking anchor of the *Esperança*. A few natives proceeded to carry our baggage, which was plentiful, up an elevation, wading through the soft mud. The proprietor, Colonel Pedro Paixão, wasn't on the premises but out collecting revenues for some roads he had put through. He wouldn't be expected back until late afternoon. Lobato, the bookkeeper, smiled wetly, undertaking to welcome the guests. Vaez assisted the girls down the gangplank, and I was lifted off under the watchful supervision of our Captain Soares, who seemed to be hoping that my soul would rest in peace. Trucco, still aboard, went to advise the American that there was no further reason to remain cooped up in his cabin, and heard a voice answer that everything was okay.

Miss Rose and Miss Constance

Michael was not at all okay and would not come out of the cabin of his own free will. The vision of Justine, her white body and its shameful practice, left him excited. And this shamed him. . . . He saw the face of Constance moaning with pleasure, and his own mother indignant with the impertinence of his fantasies. Kennedy was slowly deteriorating in his berth.

In the Heart of the Heart of the Jungle

We walked for half an hour through marshy, mossy Brazil-nut groves, until we spotted the "big house" of the Versailles Plantation. It was situated in a carefully gardened clearing. A huge two-story wood-and-stucco dwelling, encircled by a verandah which seemed to be sheltering quite an excessive number of hammocks. Looking from up on the verandah itself and out toward the river, I could still see the *Esperança*, weighing her anchor and heading for Puerto Alonso, some two hours hence along the river. I went on into the house, spacious but still lacking enough accommodations for all of us. Houses in the Amazon generally were poorly laid out, and visitors to rubber plantations made for rare occasions indeed. Lobato had prepared a room for our women and we would sleep on the verandah.

Frontier Frugality

The big house was a true example of colonial architecture. On the upper floor, the seignorial accommodations; on the lower floor, the storeroom with its piles of rubber, animal skins, Brazil nuts, piassava fiber, and gumwood. The colonel's living quarters consisted of a dining room, a study, a room for the bookkeeper, an alcove, and a spare room of no particular use and set aside for guests—hence,

for the visiting French girls. The remaining employees of
the plantation proper—overseers and revenue collectors—
lived in a string of fallen-down shacks, of wood and
thatch, located behind the big house and together forming
a kind of medieval hamlet around a central square, also
named Versailles.

The Wheels of History

Thaumaturgo Vaez had already lifted more than ten
toasts to honor the coincidence. That jungle settlement,
crisscrossed by beaten paths and bordered by tottering
huts, appeared to him to be a good omen. Versailles, the
historical plaza of the French Revolution, would be our
own point of departure. I provided the motives for several
more toasts by announcing that we would take Puerto
Alonso on July 14th.

Acrean Hospitality

Colonel Pedro Paixão and his band of hired roughnecks
arrived toward the end of a rainy afternoon. He was
mounted on a gray horse that seemed about to dissolve
in the tempest. The gunmen dispersed along the Praça
Versailles, and only the colonel came in to greet us—with
his wife, Dona Vitória, and a boy to provide us with any
needed domestic service. The colonel was thoroughly exhausted, and his sixty years no longer presented the stam-
ina of old. A trip on horseback through the jungle was
something fatiguing enough for men of younger age.
Paixão embraced Vaez, of whom he was especially fond,
given their occasional sprees in Manaus together. He
shook my hand vigorously and told me what a great com-
fort it was to finally receive visitors in that isolated spot.

Brazilian Popular Culture

Dinner was served early, on the huge jacaranda-wood
table. At the head, the colonel made his heavy, dark-
complected, deep-voiced presence warmly known to all of

us. He pampered the French *artistes* with a typical well-assorted menu of thoroughly exotic dishes, served on utterly civilized Italian porcelain. Dona Vitória supervised the table, trying to remain cordial to the guests around her. Truthfully, however, she felt little sympathy for any of us city-bred intruders, and much less for the French *mesdames* in our company. She herself was a short, dark, strong woman with perfect white teeth, the most discreet wife in all of Acre at fifty years of age. A devoted Catholic, every Sunday she would gather the ladies for a weekly pilgrimage all the way in to Puerto Alonso, to attend eight-o'clock mass. Dona Vitória saw the plantation as a species of refuge from the vices of Manaus. She felt terribly happy in that big house, on the banks of the river where she was born, and with the slow passage of time there, which had taught her to make the best of Paixão's notorious excesses. In Manaus, they had a comfortable mansion on the Rua do Barroso, occupied by their two irreverent sons, whom she no longer understood.

Brazilian Popular Culture (Revisited)

My troops would occupy the Versailles Plantation for two weeks, the period of time it finally took to convince Colonel Paixão to support the Revolution. The drinks from our commissary were definitely to the liking of the colonel, who seemed amazed at the courage of our French intelligence officers, engaged in so uncertain an undertaking. And Thaumaturgo supplied him with extensive reports on the latest news from Manaus. There were days of sun and others of rain. On the nights of heavier rain, the zinc roof of the verandah beat like telegraph keys, and kerosene lamps yellowed the dining room's interior. Dona Vitória, aloof as always, would defend to the last her besieged tranquillity.

The Origins of Rebellion in the Tropics

Each day we summoned the General Staff out onto the verandah. Dona Vitória would discreetly abandon our company and retire into the kitchen. Vaez and I together would try to elaborate our plans before Paixão, the better to gain his support. I knew that the road to the fall of Puerto Alonso passed directly through the gates of Versailles. Pedro Paixão was a natural leader, not only by virtue of the economic power he wielded, but by his appealing manner and conspicuous use of common sense. He had lived in Acre since 1833, and gained the reputation of a wise counselor.

Vaez greatly perfected my own simple arguments. I confess I was never particularly persuasive when it came to politics, but my poet friend was positively vibrant, stretching the facts, trying to allay any fears and emphasize the certainties. This, while Paixão argued that Bolivia might attempt serious reprisals; and he didn't believe in any assurances from Brazil, given that the federal government was always liquidationist in Acrean matters. Besides which, a revolution would cause the still graver problem of a significant drop in the production of rubber and other jungle commodities.

The Birth of the Opposition in the Tropics

The days went by and we saw no progress. Paixão continued to consume all our liquor while denying us any assistance: withholding his arsenal, his men trained to kill, his prestige among (Brazilian) plantation owners. My Revolution was foundering in this marasmus, as my arguments were cut to shreds. That was when Vaez decided to organize a tribute to Colonel Paixão—the most significant idea that my right-hand man had ever instigated in his life. Blangis got right to work preparing a select program sprinkled with several cancans, numerous songs, and a wealth of patriotic declamation. That very night the verandah was suddenly filled with music and lights for the improvised choreography of my French forces. The inhabitants of the area were delighted to attend, and only Dona Vitória did not deign to take her place in the audience, finding solace instead at the foot of her oratory, where she prayed for the souls of all the sinners and adventurers in the world. Dona Vitória knew well enough, pressing the beads of her rosary to her bosom, that the days of harmony in Puerto Alonso, as well as in her own home, were ended. And she could do nothing: she had learned only to be submissive in matters of politics, that decidedly masculine subject. But it was difficult for her to watch all that life of tranquillity suddenly disappear without at least trying to make an effort to avoid it. Some means must be found to expel those loose women, those inveterate alcoholics, from the company of her husband. Without knowing it, in the span of a single rosary, Dona Vitória had become the pioneer spirit in the opposition movement that would one day topple my Empire.

On the Mutability of the Will

Pedro Paixão was instantly converted, with not the slightest inkling that at that very moment so was his wife, into a political activist. But a revolution with such lovely-looking legs, with such genteel *mesdames*, certainly merited his support. That common sense, so well tempered when it came to the dangerous questions of territoriality, was now pointing vigorously to the necessity of having a hand in the Revolution. Which demonstrated to me the libertarian strength of the arts, embodied by Les Comédiens Tropicals.

The next morning, with eager rejoicing, we signed the historic document by which the colonel committed himself to throwing all his support behind the Revolution, placing even his personal staff in the category of enlistees, under my direct command. I stared up at the ceiling embroidered with spiderwebs and meditated upon the mysteries and conceits of politics in the tropics. Here were men so isolated and sad that they always felt relegated to anonymity. And there is no man of any degree of financial power who desires complete anonymity. Politics, therefore, was the stimulus that finally ignited this region of solitude that represented nothing more than the self-love of the *nouveaux riches*.

THE EMPEROR OF THE AMAZON

Ideology of Monoculture I

A collection of well-rehearsed legs clad in lace stockings, a few cancan numbers, and plenty of good liquor proved to be as persuasive an ideological argument as any other.

Ideology of Monoculture II

Politics in the tropics is really a question of choreography.

Ideology of Monoculture III

The ruling class in the tropics is ashamed of nothing.

Ideology of Monoculture IV

To be violent in the tropics is simply a question of temperament.

Puerto Alonso

Michael Kennedy forgot tropical diseases for a few moments as he examined the balance sheets of the Bolivian Delegation in Acre. He saw that the profits were truly spellbinding. He accordingly promised direct aid from the United States, in return for small customs favors. My French spies were already on hand, actively participating in the same discovery. Two Englishmen, passing themselves off as ministers of God, also offered financial assistance to the Bolivians. But there was no movement of enemy troops, and there remained in the city merely that small detachment of militia. The road was clear.

Joan of Arc

Joana had organized a battalion of latex workers and commanded her men with a fist of iron. She had learned much from the teachings of the Catholic Church. To me she hardly said a word, offering only looks of reproach. The method of extraction of the signature of adherence from Paixão was, for Joana, an *a priori* reading of the nature of my Revolution.

Order of the Day

FROM: General Vaez
TO: Marshal Galvez
Sir: Presently at Versailles are seventy rubber gatherers, recruited and transported from various centers. Training and maneuvers are proceeding normally. Versailles is well on the road to war.

> Long Live the Revolution!
> Long Live Independent Acre!
> Thaumaturgo Vaez, Brigadier General

Dispatches

The Field Marshall, utilizing his legal prerogatives, resolves:
1) To authorize the rank of Major General for Colonel Pedro Paixão, with a titulary salary of $600 per month.
2) To authorize the rank of sergeant for the following citizens: Libério Pereira (overseer), Severino Nogueira (overseer), Roberval Ladeira (ditto), and Emerentino Soares (the same), each with a monthly salary of $160.

147

So be it.
Long Live the Revolution!
Long Live Independent Acre!
Luiz Galvez Rodrigues de Aria,
Field Marshal and Supreme Commander
    of the Revolution

Another Official Communiqué

FROM: Chief Commissary Officer
TO: Marshal Galvez
Sir: This commissariat hereby solicits authori-
zation to proceed with the purchase of the
following merchandise:
  a) 3 meters of white linen
  b) 1 meter of blue linen
Purpose: manufacture of a flag for the future
Independent State of Acre.
                Long Live the Revolution!
                Long Live Independent Acre!
                José Fernando, Chief Officer

Our Flag of Worship

Justine and Joana duly fabricated our flag, according
to a design by Blangis. The General Staff lauded and
approved the design itself, with the following dispatch
especially written for the occasion by our poet-soldier
Vaez: "It is a rectangle much like the worthy and un-
worthy flags of all nations and peoples. The blue stripe,
which takes up half your field, softens the rigors of your
sumptuous nature, heralding the spirits of poets and laborers among your people. The other half, pure white:
that lily of all colors shining in one alone. White: once
again reflecting the purity of wisdom in your humble people. Firmly fixed amid these two heraldic manifestations
of peace and harmony, fulgurates a solitary star—sublime
beacon bright as our hope—lighting our way to the future.
And finally, three sacred words, arisen in the world from
the blessed lips of the ordinary people in the streets: LIB-
ERTY, EQUALITY, and FRATERNITY!"

True Adventures Can Be Dangerous

The battalion commanded by Joana and suitably dubbed the Freedom Brigade paraded elegantly around the Praça Versailles. They were skinny, toothless hicks, with straw hats and latex shoes. Yet they held their rifles with a certain grace, and three *fusiliers* demonstrated their capable marksmanship on targets in the nearby woods. I decided to enlist the three as my personal bodyguards.

From Puerto Alonso arrived the news that the Bolivians would sign a bilateral accord with Brazil, formally annexing the Territory of Acre and reclassifying the Brazilian properties therein. This reclassification consisted of the option between receiving an indemnification from the state or allowing that such holdings be catalogued as enclaves of national security. Pedro Paixão was deeply impressed by the news.

The Metaphysics of Aristotle

In Acre, annually, eight out of twenty children died in the first days of life; 20% of the active population suffered from tuberculosis; 15% from leprosy. Another 60% were infected with diseases typical of an undernourished condition; 80% of the population was illiterate. There were no doctors in Acre. A kilo of coffee cost twenty centavos. And 40% of the finest rubber in the Amazon came from Acrean territory.

PART FOUR

*July through December
of 1899,
in the Empire of Acre*

Hereupon, one finds that Art—from a lowliness of style—results in discomfort, and the king enters the comedy for the fool.

—Lope de Vega, ON THE NEW ART OF COMEDY
IN OUR TIME

Numerology

How long does a man really live? On the average, a man lives 613,200 hours of existence. But are all those hours truly lived? One can hardly be called alive during sleep, which already eliminates half our existence. And if we similarly discount the hours of routine activity, how much will still be left? In all, a man lives those moments in which he participates to the fullest in life, and in this sense life is fleeting to say the very least.

The man who writes to you, gentle reader, is a man who lived only 17,520 hours of existence. Such were the few intense hours that have dominated my life like the signal to fire on the flesh of a condemned man. I know that this may seem ridiculous, but the truth is that aside from those two years spent in the Amazon, my life has passed for little more than the tiresome outgrowth of those single moments of adventure. I lived out my adventure, and then became a legend.

The Fall of Puerto Alonso

We traversed the silence of early morning, taking advantage of the darkness. The grand moment was approaching, and I felt tense with expectation. Within a few hours my destiny would explode into being. The river was calm and our canoes glided noiselessly. I had decided to take the town with a single assault, just at the moment when its inhabitants would be awakening. I had ordered our departure for four in the morning, and the General Staff to divide our troops into three battalions, commanded by Paixão, Vaez, and Joana respectively. I calculated that by leaving Versailles at four o'clock, we would reach the town by six, when the sun would already be lighting the streets for us. We had endlessly debated the plan of attack, which

153

now seemed to be perfect to me. Our battalions would arrive at Puerto Alonso, hit the beaches, surround the Bolivian police headquarters, seizing the militiamen and dominating the key points of the town itself, and then immediately hold a rally in the main plaza. Given that the enemy presence was ridiculous, I hoped the element of surprise would avoid useless bloodshed.

Some Unexpected Surprises

The day began to grow light, Puerto Alonso already visible with its houses heaped on the edge of a bluff overlooking the river, holding back the jungle. Joana's battalion began to disembark, in order to advance along one flank of the woods, while Paixão led his men farther south, crossing in front of the town. At my side, Vaez was scanning the city with binoculars, and began to stammer that we had fallen into a trap. I took the binoculars and discovered that a well-disciplined troop was busy marching in the plaza, stepping to the brisk cadence of a military band. The uniforms they wore were of a dark, European cut, definitely not Bolivian. I pondered that it might be an army of mercenaries, in the pay of the Bolivian Syndicate. A trick of Trucco's, who had only apparently let himself be led along, the better to amuse himself with us. My expectations had suddenly taken a turn for the worse. And I was not in a position to even lament the fact, given that I was at the moment stage center. I ordered our forces to approach in the quietest manner possible, to at least keep some elements of surprise in our favor. The mercenaries, or whatever they might be, seemed not to be expecting any attack, not having posted any sentinels or patrols.

Revolutionary Impulse

It was exactly six a.m. when I ordered the assault on Puerto Alonso. The encirclement had been completed in fine time, and I made a point of being in the vanguard of the troops, disembarking on the run toward some warehouses. An avalanche of inebriates, ballet dancers, and

Cearensians fell upon the plaza, putting the contingent of totally unprepared mercenaries to a shameful rout. Left on the field of honor were their flags, standards, and musical instruments. We had achieved the first objective, without having fired a shot. Joana's Freedom Brigade was advancing from the rear, thus cutting off the withdrawal of the mercenaries, who fell prisoners without further resistance. Meantime, Paixão's battalion had swept the other wing of the city and was assembling more prisoners from the taking of the Bolivian police headquarters. Yet no one seemed to have flushed out Luiz Trucco or the American. The two English "missionaries," however, had both been arrested by Vaez and taken to the parish hall, where the curate (an Italian) had immediately adhered to the new *status quo*.

Duel at Sunrise

Joana's (now veteran) Freedom Fighters had already assembled the POWs in the plaza when a woman in uniform began to scream hysterically, brandishing a parasol at Blangis. It was the colonel from the Salvation Army, advancing against the Frenchman who had destroyed her shawl, back in Belém. She had never forgotten her forced landing on those bunches of ripe bananas, and now suddenly had reappeared, bellowing like a bull. Blangis, remembering his classes in fencing at the school of dramatic art, gallantly defended himself, deftly relieving the colonel of successive layers of her clothing. He was armed with a rapier and the scene itself was not the most edifying, to be sure. The membership of the Salvation Army—seeing their superior officer affronted in such a manner, and only in her underclothes, fencing with a portly lunatic—quickly lost all composure and, forgetting that vengeance is a sin, began to wrestle with the band of Cearensians who were busy cheering on Blangis and otherwise amusing themselves with the foray. What, in point of fact, was being enacted at the moment was the conflict that History would remember as the Pitched Battle of Puerto Alonso, which left my army victorious and became the fundamental mark of my Imperium.

THE EMPEROR OF THE AMAZON

L'Ancien Régime

I myself caught Michael Kennedy and Luiz Trucco, and led them, hands on head, over to the office of the Bolivian police department. They had naturally been attracted by all the clamor of the celebrated Pitched Battle, and had run to the plaza caught up in the crowd, curious about the sudden hubbub at an hour normally reserved for somnolent faces and indolent layabeds. The shouting that came from the plaza would, of course, have awakened anybody's curiosity in a town where only the frogs and birds manifested a similar degree of energy and enthusiasm. The two diplomats had therefore met one another while observing the scuffle from the steps of the church, without in the least comprehending the extraordinary participation of that group of uniformed members of the normally pacific Salvation Army. Yet there they were, rolling on the ground with ladies in gay-colored dresses and obviously drunken gentlemen, and both diplomats were so distracted by the melee that they failed even to recognize me until, dripping with sweat, I shoved the barrel of my Winchester into the back of Luiz Trucco, placing him and his American companion under arrest. Yet I cannot accuse them of acting imprudently, because a duel between a rapier and a parasol is, even to this day, rather uncommon—especially one pitting a lady colonel of the Salvation Army against a gentleman conductor of Italian opera.

Illusions of Reality

From the perspective that time affords, that duel was no more strange than the rest of my Revolution. The letter that Luiz Trucco composed later on, once he was safely in Manaus (where I would finally order him to be sent), really contained very little of what had actually taken place on that morning. A letter addressed to Minister Aramayo, the Bolivian ambassador stationed in London and principal spokesman for the Bolivian Syndicate.

156

International Repercussions

Lack of imagination in Luiz Trucco would still not prevent an explosive outburst on the part of the volatile minister of temeritous whiskers. Upon reading the objective, detailed description of the text in question, the latter would tear down all the velvet drapes in his chamber and sweep with a hairy fist the altogether cluttered surface of his writing desk. And on that same night, his blood still boiling, Aramayo would refuse to touch the same copy of The London *Times* just leafed through (*estuprado!*), moments before, by the peaceable Brazilian ambassador (a Carioca from a good family, who probably didn't even know where Acre was), thereby provoking an unfortunate pall among the members of the Escort Club (habitual haunt of diplomats from "those exotic lands," as they were dubbed by Buckingham Palace).

Historical Facts

The Pitched Battle of Puerto Alonso lasted exactly ninety minutes, judiciously timed by our chief medic, Dr. Nobre. Once the dust had cleared, the crumpled Soldiers of Christ were bemoaning the dents in their musical instruments in near-perfect harmony to the laments of French *legionnaires*, who had likewise incurred a few indecently placed scratches, not to mention several black eyes and field dresses irreparably torn in strategic locations. To be honest, Blangis had wound up on the losing end, soundly defeated by the well-managed umbrella of the lady colonel. Dr. Nobre attended to the wounds with two liters of tincture of arnica and lots of bandage.

Illustrious Prisoners

At the Bolivian police station, held incommunicado, were the American consul, Trucco, six militiamen from Bolivia, and all the visiting dignitaries. I ordered a detachment of Freedom Fighters to stand guard over the prisoners.

Rally

The whole population of Puerto Alonso was out on the streets, awakened by the battle, jamming the plaza with children around their necks, the old, the infirm, even household pets. I ordered the Bolivian flag to be lowered, and then—with a lyric from Aida, to lend the ceremony a solemn air—the Acrean standard was hoisted. Vaez's troops cleared a space around the flagpole, trying to contain the multitude. Then we proceeded to enter the plaza, mounted on pitiful-looking pintos actually decked out for the Feast of the Holy Spirit, held every June, and to an improvised choreographic accompaniment of Blangis's invention. Parading beside me were Generals Pedro Paixão and Thaumaturgo Vaez. We were immediately surrounded by the masses, and I began to observe those ragged men and their mistreated women, old and pregnant. My subjects depressed me. . . . From the top of the flagpole fluttered the flag of the Revolution.

"Your Tired and Your Poor"

My subjects observed everything in their own way. They were curious, but could not appreciate the significance of the event. After all, we were mounted on horseback with harnesses and trimmings out of another epoch, and this provoked rumors which were almost as quickly discredited. A people who always submitted to the facts, to events themselves, when they could not quite manage to grasp the same, they muttered rumors. Some believed that I was Dom Pedro I, returning from the grave to the throne of Brazil. Or perhaps the lost Sebastian. . . . They had always lived in that limbo of undertones, simulating a false passivity. The same passivity with which they had received the bearer of fiery tidings, when first approached by him back in the Northeast; or the same as when they watched their companions dying of diarrhea on the long march to some mythical place called Acre. And so they murmured, even as their own debts filled the coffers of the colonels. Murmurs and rumors, these were the practical ways of watching out for one's own luck, not meddling in politics. In the end, in the tropics, the politicians—like God himself—had their own unfathomable reasons.

Viva o Imperador do Acre!

Justine L'Amour was overtaken by some burlesque fit of passion, I saw when she appeared in the plaza, urging the people on, shielding her half-uncovered bust, ordering about her female cohorts as if she were making her entrance on an immense, lushly foliated stage and her cue had occurred in the exact middle of the spectacle. She lifted her arms and urged a chorus of *"Vivas!"* for the Emperor. Bursts of applause broke forth and my soldiers busily stimulated the more apathetic Acreans. Vaez and Paixão also joined in, tossing their hats into the air while shouting their own *vivas!* for the Emperor of Acre. Finally, even my subjects joined in and the curate began to set off some fireworks from the door of the church. I slowly advanced to the center of the plaza, where Blangis had set up a sort of altar with paper flowers. . . . I noticed I was holding a Bolivian sword, handed me at some point by someone I no longer remember. So I lifted the sword skyward and, with my foot in the stirrup, punctuated my words with blows in the air.

The Cry of Acre

GALVEZ: *Pátria e Liberdade! Viva o Acre Livre! Viva a Revolução!*

Geopolitics

I was freeing Acre from both Bolivian and Brazilian tutelage, forming an independent nation, exactly according to plan. . . .

THE EMPEROR OF THE AMAZON

Document for the Future

A pity not to have had a photographer available to record the moment. The one photographer in Puerto Alonso (a combination street peddler and wandering portraiteer, native of Greece) had passed away only six months prior to the event, in an unfortunate quarrel with the husband of his mistress. Later on, in a vain attempt to compensate for the omission, Blangis tried unsuccessfully to reproduce the event on an oil canvas, but with an incomplete set of paints, thus inaugurating a new mode of painting which might have been called the Acrean School. The painting itself, poorly executed, with no reds or greens and tending too much toward the blues, would be seized as evidence at the time of my deposal. It constituted Exhibit "A" at my trial and was later bought by a German tourist, at an antique auction in Rio, in the late '20s. Eventually, in 1942, it would show up again, this time at a *Strasse* in Dusseldorf, together with other considered-to-be-decadent items quickly incinerated by order of the Führer.

Second Day of a Revolution

I handed down my first decrees. In the very first, I sanctioned the founding of the Empire of Acre, delineating its precise frontiers, for which task I drew upon the geographical aptitudes of Pedro Paixão. I also signed official letters communicating the birth of my Empire to all the civilized nations of the world, and a special one to President Campos Sales, of Brazil, soliciting his understanding.

Decree

The Emperor of Acre, in his prerogatives of Sovereign and Maximum Representative of the popular will, decrees:
    1) The creation of a National Budget.

2) The confiscation of the revenues of the former Bolivian Customs Office in Puerto Alonso.
3) The transformation of the above-mentioned revenues into the previously mentioned National Budget.
4) The sum of 145,368,908$00 (*cruzeiros*) for the National Budget.

> Published & Proclaimed,
> Luiz Galvez Rodrigues de Aria
> Emperor of Acre

Arrogance of 1899

The Emperor of Acre, in his prerogatives of Sovereign and Maximum Representative of the popular will, decrees:
1) The creation of a Committee for National Salvation. And nominates:
2) Major General Pedro Paixão to be President of the above-mentioned Committee.

> Published & Proclaimed,
> Luiz Galvez Rodrigues de Aria
> Emperor of Acre

A Revolution Is a Revolution

The Emperor of Acre, in his prerogatives of Sovereign and Maximum Representative of the popular will, decrees:
ONLY PARAGRAPH: The expropriation of the property at Praça 14 de Julho, former Praça 15 de Novembro, No. 78, owned by citizen Pedro Paixão to be added to the Nation's patrimony.

> Published & Proclaimed,
> Luiz Galvez Rodrigues de Aria
> Emperor of Acre

Curt Note

Mr. Galvez:
Look here, my friend, you seem to be getting a little carried away with all this business of decrees. I think you should know that I don't take kindly to their having taken my storage facilities at Praça 15 de Novembro from me.

From your friend,
Pedro Paixão

Response

My Dear Pedro Paixão:
Rest assured that this will happen no more. The mansion which you were using as your storage depot is to be transformed into an Imperial Palace, the seat of our new government. We shall, of course, provide a handsome indemnity. And the fifty tons of rubber, which is your merchandise, were never meant to be included in the decree and remain your property. But please remember that the plaza is now called 14 de Julho, in homage to our Revolution.

Cordial Greetings,
Luiz

Palatine Priorities

In a few days, crowds of workers, prompted by the lure of rum and *cachaça*, would clean out and put into proper shape what would be known, with a profound condescension, as the Imperial Palace. This, in accordance with the orders of Blangis, charged by the Committee for National Salvation to proceed with the installation of the seat of government in a suitably worthy location.

Archaeology

Blangis was rummaging around collecting objects either set aside or no longer of use from the rubber plantations and the houses of merchants in the city. A number of interesting items had already been unearthed. An eighteenth-century Portuguese sofa with a cane seat had become a hen roost in the back of a house near the Imperial Palace, and two Chippendale chairs lay in a tool shed belonging to a merchant.

Architect and Landscape Gardener

In the mansion baptized the Imperial Palace, there was a great hall for audiences and receptions, a royal study for my exclusive use, my bed chamber, and several other alcoves divided among the French ladies and higher-ranking revolutionaries. Meals were served out in a latticework gazebo built in the back of the house, near the guava trees and jungle creepers transplanted from the forest by my able landscape architect, "maestro" Blangis.

Machiavelli and the Modern State

To avoid any further dissension, I decided to hand down a decree abolishing any tax on crude rubber, which abundantly satisfied all the proprietors in Acre. They thereby had their profits increased and Blangis had his work facilitated, so that no one seemed to mind any longer giving up a worthless eighteenth-century sofa, an Italian console table, a jacaranda desk, or anything else requisitioned by my dedicated interior decorator.

The New Regime

The ceremony for my coronation, held in the already deliriously decorated Imperial Palace and of a pomp until then unheard of at such a latitude in the tropics, was enacted with unparalleled majesty. The reader will pardon the grandiloquent style, but every coronation is thus. Blangis, the master of *papier-mâché* improvisation, came up with a truly dazzling recepton hall, including all the rococo detail of an eighteenth-century set from *Don Giovanni*. The gold leaf, the false ivory, the *trompe l'oeil*, the romantic scenes in vague hues, the curtained artifice, altogether awed the guests—veteran fighters who had accumulated their fortunes in the jungle, virtual illiterates who were now wholly intimidated by the magic of that French Merlin, capable of transforming in so few days a stinking storehouse for crude rubber into a dream palace.

Napoleon's Galoshes

During my coronation, the French girls, in gala costumes from the festival scene of the opera *Carmen*, organized an impromptu chorale and presented selected numbers from the former repertory of the Compagnie Opératique, now disbanded by misfortune. Somewhere between the strophes of a delicate *romanza* from *The Barber of Seville*, "Ecco ridente in cielo," I neglected the advice of Sir Henry and acceded to my Empire with a Napoleonic gesture. I placed upon my own head a wreath of rubber leaves molded in silver.

Crown of Rubber

My strikingly original crown was a gift from the vicar of Puerto Alonso, ever anxious to show his adherence to the new regime. It had originally been sent to Puerto Alonso as a gift of the Bolivian government, to be used in a coronation ceremony for the Virgin-Patroness of the city, who was embodied in a striking life-size plaster figure set upon the main altar of the church.

Demagoguery

I delivered a trifling address, promising to bring civilization to the shores of Acre and much justice to her people. The last part of my discourse, referring to justice and the people, escaped me in a moment of excessive enthusiasm and was of course to be taken as an evident exaggeration. I ordained the commencement of the festivities, expected to last throughout the week.

Imperial Buffet

Veuve Cliquot corks popped in the reception hall, and an orchestra put together with elements drawn from the Salvation Army—deserters who had abandoned the uniform, attracted by the *luxe* of my regime—attacked an animated polka with genuine *brio*. I ordered *cachaça*, cookies, and chunks of pork to be distributed to the populace congregating at the entrance to the Palace.

Premonition

The manner with which my subjects received the brandy, and the avidity with which they threw themselves into the plates of food, permitted me to have a fair idea of the ideological basis of my Empire which had just installed itself.

My Beloved Dissident

Joana refused to show up for my coronation. She said that what was happening in Acre was a total travesty and that I would pay dearly for it. But I didn't take Joana's outrage too seriously; she would always remain a faithful friend, if push came to shove, though she stormed out of my study when I promised to hand down a decree authorizing the title of Baroness of Acre for her. That same day, she boarded a vessel and headed for the Upper Acre, a region still not in the hands of the Bolivians and bastion of those merchants now hostile to Pedro Paixão.

The Stronger Sex

I have the impression today that Joana considered herself the person most appropriate to effect a revolution in

Acre. In one of those bitter conversations I had with her, she referred to the unjust position of women in the patriarchal society based upon latex. Pedro Paixão was around at the time and answered that he thought the position of women was quite adequate as it was, for those who did no more than cook food and bear children. But Joana was not referring to this species of queen bee or mother hen which Paixão saw in women. She went about now in quite masculine garb—without losing her feminine charm, I might add. I felt myself wholly seduced by the figure of Joana in the work clothes of the *seringueiro*, her curves boldly accentuated by the cartridge belts and masterly gait of her campaign boots. She was a modern Amazon woman with no need to extirpate one of her breasts to prove it; she preferred to attack masculine society from the same camp as Venus.

A Woman from Another Epoch

At a time when women merely menstruated, conceived, and gave birth, without troubling themselves about their condition, Joana was a conscience exposed like a nerve. Acremoniously so. . . .

The Royal Ball of Puerto Alonso

Let us continue with the coronation. The deserters from the Salvation Army, though they may have been bad Christians, formed a spirited orchestra. The food was bounteous and the liquor was superb: the first moments of luxury and euphoria in my Imperium. From my throne I could observe the celebration, which little by little was degenerating into an orgy. The long reception hall, brightly illuminated by candelabras, was as enlivened as its decor. Guests were becoming more and more uninhibited. The two longer walls, both without windows, were dressed with murals in the taste of Louis Philippe, depicting the Arc de Triomphe, the Seine, and women of the 1880s. At the extreme opposite end from my throne, the main entryway opened between two niches where plaster-of-Paris cupids stretched gilded bows. On a wooden dais and contrasting with the rococo pomp was the orchestra, in costumes from the opera *Semiramide* and struggling to be heard above the din of voices. My inebriated subjects were trying to get their hands on a few women and smudging the paper scenography with sweat. General Pedro Paixão, who had obviously not come with Dona Vitória, lay prostrate between two Creoles, stretched out on a sofa and staring bleary-eyed at the miraculous walls which seemed to be dissolving.

Taste of Civilization

Whoever peered closely at the reception hall would have noticed an unmistakable air of the slaughterhouse in all the bodies piled upon one another amid pools of vomit and sweat. Hair and shreds of *papier-mâché* fluttering in the air. François Blangis could hardly have been able to lament the spoilage, however, given his condition, stretched out flat in back of the orchestra in a profound unconsciousness. Just outside my Imperial Palace, another orchestra of a more regional flavor refused to give in. A populace who had never experienced the delights of a coronation let themselves go, around and around the huge bonfires.

Under the Sign of Utopia

The whole thing made me want to take a walk, and I escaped for a few minutes from that banquet hall steamy enough to have been mistaken for a Finnish sauna. I walked through the rows of guests and stepped out into the plaza, where women and their men in tatters—skinny and innocent—were singing in what appeared to me rather constrained voices of enthusiasm. So these were my subjects, I asked myself once again, as if the idea still appeared totally unreal to me. I took another look at the beardless faces; at the few women of bony frame, rotted teeth, and sweaty clothes; smelled the *cachaça*; heard the murmuring voices that brought to mind a far different idea from that of subjects. But between the slaughterhouse behind me and the Good Samaritanism that now crossed my mind, I would have preferred to be alone with a good Frascati. I tried to get away from all that, quickly.

I walked over to the former Bolivian police headquarters, where Luiz Trucco was still imprisoned, awaiting my deliberation. I opened the door and saw the old fellow, his white head and tired eyes, reading his Anatole France under the watchful eyes of two half-breeds. He looked up, and must have noticed that I was drunk and my clothes were soaked with sweat. A look of recrimination and profound contempt, as it could not otherwise have been. The noise of celebration floated in the background like a distant thunder, and the figure of Trucco himself seemed enclosed in a wall of glass. Still holding my goblet of wine, I lifted a toast in his direction and then downed the contents. I knew (in my drunken lucidity) that the pallor of that old man, like the orgy itself, was but the first gray cloud prelusive to the storm. The melancholy light of the single flickering candle made the walls quiver, and the smell of must was overpowering. I locked the door behind me and returned to the reception hall, climbing the shaky wooden steps at the back of the house, and I entered that lingering decay of pouchy scrotums and taut nipples. With no longer a vestige of music, beyond the monotonous howl of voluptuousness, as if from a single throat. And bodies glued to the last remnants of effaced murals in moist spasms.

Launching an Administration

The Emperor of Acre, in his prerogatives of Sovereign and Maximum Representative of the popular will, conscious of the need to get the task of normalization underway, resolves:

1) To create a Cabinet to replace the provisional Committee for National Salvation.
2) To convoke a Constituent Assembly to elaborate the juridical features of the nation.

Published & Proclaimed,
Luiz Galvez Rodrigues de Aria
Emperor of Acre

Illustrious Names

The Emperor of Acre, in his prerogatives of Sovereign, resolves:

ONLY PARAGRAPH: To name the citizens below to the corresponding cabinet posts, likewise enumerated:

MINISTER OF EDUCATION: Joana Ferreira

MINISTER OF HEALTH: Dr. Amarante Nobre de Castro

MINISTER OF FOREIGN RELATIONS: Thaumaturgo Vaez

MINISTER OF CULTURE: François Blangis

MINISTER OF WAR: General Pedro Paixão

MINISTER OF JUSTICE AND THE INTERIOR: Felismino de Sá, Esq.

Illustrious Anonyms I

The reader has yet to hear me speak of Attorney Felismino, to whom I nonetheless delegated so important a post in my Cabinet. Well, let me tell you, then, that he was educated in the state of Pernambuco as a specialist in commercial law, even though he made his living in Manaus as a civil attorney, protesting titles and foreclosing mortgages. Felismino was also a tireless frequenter of the Hotel Cassina, and a grand connoisseur of wines. In short, he never gave me any problem.

Illustrious Anonyms II

As for my Minister of War, the more than deserving ex-Colonel Pedro Paixão, he was the only case of a rubber general in the whole history of the Amazon.

Illustrious Anonyms III

Attorney Felismino da Sá was also the author of a volume of poetry, entitled *Parchments of Autumnal Twilight*.

Illustrious Anonyms IV

The first task undertaken by the Minister of Health was to cure the Emperor of one hell of a hangover. He gave me a preparation made from guaraná which I still consider a saintly remedy. I now reveal to the reader Dr. Nobre's secret cure for a hangover:

Guaraná powder .... 5 to 20 grams.
Pyramidon .... 10 to 40 grams.
For one capsule.

Important: the guaraná has to be grated with the tongue of a pirarucu fish.

Guaraná

Guaraná works well after a hangover both as a sedative and as a tranquilizer. I ordered five hundred bars from Manaus.

Forgive Me, Reader!

I interrupt once again to advise that our hero has been indulging in a systematic abuse of the imagination ever since he arrived in Manaus. And how well he leads us on! Just for starters, what he actually tried to initiate, in Acre, was a Liberal Republic. And furthermore . . . well . . . as a matter of fact, thinking it over, why spoil it for the reader?

Acrean Florilegium

Thaumaturgo Vaez started to write a grand epic poem celebrating the conquest of Acre and the founding of its Empire.

Márcio Souza

My Bland Century

Ah, 1899! Besides my hallucinatory Empire, lost in the middle of the jungle like some forgotten utopia of Campanella, future historians will have a great deal to talk about concerning that year. Days of gaiety, wretchedness, and (of course) pomp during which men busily prepared for a new century of tremendous changes. And perhaps because of the latter, the approaching 1900s would come to be imprecisely known as *modern* times. England was suffering humiliating difficulties in the war against the Boers, in Africa. Her immense colonial empire was threatening to crumble, yet the nobility would still blithely parade along Kensington Road in gilded carriages, rejoicing over the liberation of Mafeking as if they had rid the earth of a new barbarism. For the humbler members of the planet, however, life was pretty much the same as always: exhaustive hours of work and pitiful wages, in humble contrast to the plentiful tables of the petty bourgeoisie. My Acrean subjects, too, were playing their own part in this latest, inauspicious flip of civilization's coin. And if my regime seemed to promise little in the way of bettering the situation, changes were nevertheless taking place in Puerto Alonso.

Lost City

Before the much applauded Pitched Battle had taken place, the principal topics of conversation in Puerto Alonso were confined to the latest quotations for rubber on the international market, the subtleties of flood and ebb tide along the river, and the innocuous gossip of inoffensive families. With the arrival of my *très jolies* gendarmes, the gay parades of my inebriated army, the gala occasions at the Imperial Palace, the plentiful supply of free *cachaça*, the city seemed to gain new blood in its tired veins. Finally, even the papers in Manaus were attesting to the growing importance of Acre, and my subjects took great pride in the fact.

THE EMPEROR OF THE AMAZON

Imperial Routine

François Blangis, armed with his prerogatives of Minister of Culture, never ceased to concern himself with the unfortunate appearance of the city. After all, any court worthy of its name would hardly endure streets of mud or the total absence of any nocturnal diversions (obliging even Ministers of State to retire to bed with the chickens!). Blangis dreamed of an opera house even more opulent than the Teatro Amazonas. He dreamed of Puerto Alonso's one day becoming a model metropolis, with all the modern conveniences which had so astonished visitors to the Electric Pavilion at the Paris Exposition of 1899. Every morning, accompanied by his makeshift staff of idealistic young girls, recruited from among the more innocent sectors of the populace, my Minister of Culture would set out on foot to cross the distance that separated his house from the Imperial Palace. Blangis was irked, of course, by the inconvenience of a minister's being obliged to expose himself like an ordinary citizen each day in the streets, and felt the ideal would have been to use a landau drawn by four horses—preferably white ones—or even one of those daring new steam- or combustion-driven carriages that so thrilled the streets of London, lately. Blangis's impatience, however, was uncalled for: there was nothing to expedite, nor any cultural activities to try his patience.

Hot Line

My General Paixão had retired to Versailles, and from there would daily communicate with the Palace by means of an expensive telegraph apparatus expropriated from the Bolivians, which Vaez had discovered over a year ago, crated in the back of police headquarters. The telegraph would remain inactive through most of the day, but begin to function frenetically after five p.m. The telegraph operator would transmit the heated inquiries from Paixão as to the nocturnal programming of the Palace. Our after-dinner activity was the only spark capable of igniting Paixão's interest in the latest news from Puerto Alonso.

Of the Expedient

With the early arrival of the Minister of Culture at the Imperial Palace, the day's administrative activity could be considered to be underway, even if I were only to lend my august presence much later—say, just prior to lunch—and as long as I wasn't in a bad mood and didn't have a hangover. My entrance was always festive; representative groups of subjects from the various provinces, wearing Sunday clothes and accompanied by regional musicians, would come forward to offer their humble gifts. Some gifts, of course, weren't quite so humble, and Justine L'Amour slowly accumulated an extravagant wardrobe of fanciful leather garb. With this collection, she would make a small fortune subsequent to the fall of my Empire.

Herculean Task

The police department was the only sector of my administration which seemed to be overburdened by work. Breaking the long tradition of being a peaceable city, Puerto Alonso now manifested a high incidence of disorderly conduct. The unparalleled consumption of liquor was provoking constant misunderstandings which almost always resulted in fatal—or at least irreversible—consequences. Wives were being battered by dissatisfied husbands inflamed by *cachaça*. Frequent crowds of young *seringueiros* would suddenly explode in the dockside taverns. The body of a nameless drifter was found bobbing in the river. Every sort of fevered activity began to find its way into the yellowed, empty pages of the local police blotter.

Frontier Rumblings

Joana returned from the Upper Acre and warned me of a possible uprising against my government, organized by the plantation owner Neutel Maia, allied with the Bolivians. I dispatched two scouts to the Upper Acre, with the mission of keeping my government informed of developments.

THE EMPEROR OF THE AMAZON

Matutinal Voluptuary

After his timely arrival at the Imperial Palace, my Minister of Culture would sit out in the florid gazebo, surrounded by secretaries while awaiting the appearance of the rest of my Cabinet. A pasha encircled by tawny-skinned odalisques. . . . Blangis had likewise become a great friend of the poet Vaez, to whom he would elaborate his ridiculously farfetched and grandiose plans with the imaginative voluptuousness that only the breakfast hour could provide. From one of these divagations without immediate hope of realization came the idea of constructing an Imperial Palace truly worthy of a progressive nation the likes of Acre. Assisted by his ecstatic secretaries, who quickly provided him with brush and paper, Blangis drew up an architectonic prospectus that left the poet Vaez definitively enthralled with the creative brillance of his colleague, the Minister of Culture. For those who knew Blangis, however, that Babylonic vision in gouache was hardly anything new. Its model, the incredibly expensive set for *The Marriage of Figaro* by Mozart—hence the markedly eighteenth-century flavor—had been rejected years ago, in Europe, for exceeding the budget of the opera company.

Cellar in Jeopardy

Good drinks were getting scarce in the Empire of Acre. I discovered as much one morning when I opened my eyes and the world seemed nothing but a splitting headache. The day penetrated my eyes with blinding cruelty. I handed down an order for my Cabinet to come up with some decent drinks for the Imperial cellar. *Cachaça* might be just, for my subjects, but not for the Sun King himself.

Dialogues from the Third World I

I was scowling like a true Latin American dictator. A woman of the people was speaking. The chief of police had already dozed off.

WOMAN: Oh, you excellency, my husband din't wanna listen to me and din't wanna come home no more at night, no sir. . . . So I tolt him: if'n you doan get your tail home soon I'm going over there'n turn you into a capon. See, you excellency, he was makin' time wit some cheap hoor, if you know what I mean. . . . But he din't believe what I tolt him. So I says to myself, hell! I din't get no orders from mama to take that kine da shit from him. . . . I got my honor, doan I? So I marched over while he's asleep and ketched him. An' I din't discuss matters, no sir, I slit his cockles like a capon, jus like I said I's goin to: if he ain' mine, he ain' nobody else's neither, cause I ain' about to run aroun havin my kits groan up with no man aroun' the house, no sir, you excellency.

Literature

It's incredible how the Brazilian people can possess such an innate sense of current trends in language. And yet, even with a solid background in Zola to draw upon, I find myself at a loss to reproduce it.

Dialogues from the Third World II

GALVEZ: What steps have been taken?
CHIEF OF POLICE: . . . ?!
GALVEZ: What steps, man?
CHIEF OF POLICE: Well, um . . . (yawn) Actually, the victim couldn't sustain the wound, he died. Dr. Nobre ascribed the death to a severe hemorrhage, it says so on the death certificate, right there. . . . She goes off to jail. The problem, though, is the kids.
GALVEZ: Kids? How many?
CHIEF OF POLICE: There's eleven of them, all told. The biggest is twelve years old.
GALVEZ: Release the woman at once! And look here, widow, you're not to go around severing any more scrotums, you understand? I'm going to let you off this time, but you see to those kids. . . . Audience closed!

The Decline of the West

My Empire was an absurd bit of world with its laws so resembling a state of nature. Viewed at a certain distance, it might well have pleased some philosopher of the Enlightenment. A world of precarious equilibrium where, through my adventure, I had provoked changes. Yet for me, that apparent peace—the seeming facility with which my Empire had been installed—was far worse than a prolonged and foolish war might have been, even in those treacherous everglades that constituted the bulk of my coveted territory.

I had great difficulties in coming to any understanding with my explosive subjects. Just to maintain a conversation with that woman who appeared to be sixty, but who was well under forty and spoke of her crime as if she had stolen a piece of candy, was for me a burden and a sacrifice. My audiences with representatives of the people themselves were always a fiasco. They were persons with whom I had had minimal contact in my life, and I slowly discovered that the wretched of the earth moved about in a subterranean world with laws of its own. Wretchedness, too, establishes its own confraternity.

Problems of Incarceration

Dr. Nobre informed me that the health of the American consul had reached a delicate state. The Minister of War, therefore, decided to charter a transport and dispatch the prisoner to Manaus. Luiz Trucco would travel in the same vessel. Michael Kennedy had begun to speak in a child's voice, would sit for hours like a dingy rag doll in his canvas chair, and wet himself whenever he spotted Justine in the vicinity. Trucco, who had maintained a surprising dignity as prisoner of war, could no longer endure living in the same atmosphere as the American. He pleaded for an urgent transfer to another prison, where he might be free from such continual vexation. Beyond the repugnance he felt to see that example of well-educated human being soiling himself in so cowardly a fashion, Trucco refused to accept being obliged to change his companion's clothes, as if he were changing diapers. The ex-majordomo of the American had turned to spending the entire day in a drunken stupor, and apparently also had come to terms with a Bolivian woman. But the final straw, which made Trucco lose all patience, was when Kennedy started to call him, during the constant changing of clothes, in a voice that appeared to plead with tearfully blue eyes, by the affectionate name of Miss Rose. To be confounded with the tramp of Kennedy's adolescence was the supreme insult which I had indirectly managed against Trucco's person.

Safe Conduct

Informed of the unusual turn of events, I immediately signed the order and took it upon myself to personally supervise the embarkation of my chief enemies. Boarding the steamship, though, Trucco directed at me a terrible peal of laughter that made everyone think he had somehow contracted the same malady as the poor American. Luiz Trucco would never pardon me for my abuses, and even at the hour of his death, in an attack of irreverent apoplexy—on an afternoon in Iquitos, Peru, where he was sharing his bed with a married lady—he would still mutter a final malediction against my person. And I well understood the meaning of that raucous laugh, less the fruit of madness than a sign of secret victory.

The Marriage of Figaro

Vaez and Blangis strolled about together, cogitating their idea for an Imperial Palace of true proportions. For the reader also to have some notion of what this eighth wonder of the world would be like, suffice it to say that the structure was to house three hundred bedrooms alone. The reception hall would echo the Alhambra, and the wing for Parliament would accommodate twenty thousand people. If construction were to proceed normally, it would be completed by 1970.

Thermometer

Without my perceiving it, my Empire was beginning to founder like an abandoned airship slowly deflating.

The Cabinet Deliberates

Reunion to study the feasibility of construction of the Imperial Palace. Muffled orchestra executing an *adagio* by Vivaldi. My Minister of Culture unfolds his *croquis* of the Palace like an embroideress holding up her piece of needlepoint. The immediate problem would be contracting sufficient laborers and artisans from Europe, who would certainly not wish to work in Acre. Vaez knew well enough how difficult the construction of the Teatro Amazonas had been in that respect. Blangis gave an estimate of 650,000 pounds sterling for the total cost of construction and interior decoration. I agreed to the project.

Politics of de Montesquieu

Joana was continuing with her work, irrespective of the deliriums of my Cabinet. She would meet with the people, was organizing schools, and set up recreation centers in the interior of the country. Of all my revolutionaries, she was the only one who knew our territory from end to end. She understood the problems of the nation and attempted to find ready solutions. In this way, she had painstakingly won over the confidence of the populace. Yet she was becoming more and more exhausted and discouraged. She wore cheap calico dresses and a gray uniform for solemn occasions. Her most cherished activity was to assist numbers of the masses by writing letters for them. She liked to get to know the intimacies and aspirations of her people, expressed in the missives they would write to their nearest kin. She was moved by the unwashed lies which the majority of Cearensians would invariably write. My subjects did not wish any news of their wretchedness to reach the distant homeland, and so they reaffirmed the docile illusion of ready fortunes to those they had left behind.

Márcio Souza

A Good and Well-Behaved People

I cannot complain—my people generally avoided denigrating the image of the nation abroad.

The Guerrilla Fighter

Joana did not hide the fact that her various recreational centers were a network of paramilitary organizations. She had even (secretly) requisitioned a shipment of arms and was steadily distributing rifles and ammunition to the rubber workers. She was certainly no lover of the hunt, so these arms were obviously being spread around for some possible eventuality. Yet I felt, strangely enough, a little more at ease when I saw, in the efforts of Joana, the insurrection that would immediately occur in Acre, should my government be overthrown.

December

Definitely, the winter is not the best season for an empire in the tropics. A dense drizzle had been falling for two weeks, turning Puerto Alonso into a muddy gruel. My subjects were more like worms curled up in their soppy houses. And punished by the rains, we dedicated ourselves to parlor games. The Cabinet itself had been discussing the approaching passage of the century. I had just canceled my visit to the provinces, not at all disposed to traveling in such unstable weather, particularly under jungle conditions. I knew how the jungle begins to rot from the seasonal rains, and to a good Spaniard from the Atlantic littoral, the prospective vulnerability that a constantly wet skin can offer induced only horror. Besides which, as an offspring of an admiral, I had always harbored an ancestral mistrust of tempests.

Justine and the French ladies seemed not to be troubled by the rains, except for the resulting humidity which was causing fungus rot on their clothes, their musical scores, and even their jewels. Justine actually seemed to feel much better in the closed-in atmosphere with its climate of colder nights and cooler days. Not to mention that our parlor games seemed to her a more civilized activity than swims in the channel.

Relaxation of Customs

Incidentally, there had been such swims in the channel, with wicker baskets of fried chicken spread out on wide linen tablecloths beside the river. Thus introducing a new custom—the use of bathing suits by women—and abolishing once and for all the antiquated dark dresses for genteel ladies and the slightly more revealing underslips of the prostitutes. Of course, the new swimsuits provoked considerable scandal among the womenfolk and a protest from the curate, in a sermon, on Sunday. But it was a debt that Acre had already contracted *in saecula saeculorum* with civilization. Thaumaturgo Vaez would write in his notebook of the French bathers: "Gentle clamor of Naiads in a foliant tapestry of luxuriant verdure and crystalline waters."

Ministerial Insomniac

Blangis appreciated that the passing of the century was one of those rarest of historical occasions. It was necessary, therefore, to mark it with some grand artistic exposition, something of significantly international regal proportions. Yet he was forced to desist due to lack of sufficient funds. Imagine how much Sarah Bernhardt would charge to grace Puerto Alonso with one of her Shakespearean monologues? And Caruso, think how much he would ask, just to sing a few arias! Besides which, there was the more serious problem of protecting these famous personalities from any possible tropical malaise. Michael Kennedy and Blangis' own Compagnie Opératique provided warning enough. . . . How to allow *la Bernhardt* to finish her days in a sanatorium? Or the great Caruso, must he be snuffed out by *la fièvre jaune*? And so, Blangis himself was the first to reluctantly drop his own idea, performing in the process a great service to humanity. And he restrained himself from actually communicating the idea to the more impul-

sive Vaez, who would not have hesitated to risk the very
lives of such performers.

Project for a Réveillon Didactique

Blangis sought me out to discuss his plan, with the
vehemence of a true minister. The project would also
begin to make amends for certain Acrean irregularities,
such as the rationing of decent alcoholic beverages, for
example. Blangis would order a tremendous shipment of
wines and champagne, and organize, for the 31st of December, a grand allegorical procession recounting to my
subjects the great moments of universal history. Floats and
becostumed figures would relive the epic days of Greece,
the marvels of Louis XV, the industrial revolution, the
fall of the Bastille, and the cry of Acre. The parade should
begin at precisely ten a.m., when Jupiter, in his gilded
quadriga, would bolt down the flag-draped avenue with
his retinue of libidinous deities. At noon, the nearly concluded marble staircase of the future Imperial Palace would
be ceremoniously unveiled. I might even inaugurate, later
that afternoon, the opening of one or two public schools.

More Immediate Steps

Vaez wasted no time telegraphing our embassy in Manaus, in order to arrange things. Every vagabond on the
streets of that metropolis must be recruited to serve as
actor in the parade, as well as a consolation to our own
people. And this was not to be the only shady aspect of
our business dealings with Manaus concerning the turn of
the century. A good part of the eventual liquor supply, as
well as a pyrotechnical display involving twenty thousand
salvos (a *thousand* for each century!), was carefully re-
routed to Acre.

"The Blindest of All Is He . . ."

I might easily have recognized the symptoms of the
crisis when the quotation for rubber fell, in the first weeks

of December. The winter had forced a sudden drop, and Brazil nuts were also mildewing in warehouses, worthless on the market. The landowners had begun grumbling and were prepared to blame me. I was the one responsible, not only for the drop, but for the systematic abandonment of the principal centers of latex extraction. The *seringueiros* clearly preferred the talked-about sensations of Puerto Alonso to the exhausing work of cutting. And the scholastic movement of Joana was hardly welcomed by the proprietors, almost all of them uneducated illiterates themselves.

". . . Who Looks for a Utopia"

A specially commissioned steamer docked in Puerto Alonso, to unload the shipment of merchandise for welcoming in the new century. A shipment hardly to be recommended for an empire that was already on its knees. . . . Two hundred girls of every possible pigment and for every persuasion were already disembarking with considerable effect, signaling with upheld fingers the figures they hoped to command along the docks and completely winning over the expectant populace. For this reason, perhaps, no one noticed that Sunday mass was no longer being celebrated in the city church. Dona Vitória had set up an altar in the Praça Versailles, where all her ladies were uplifting fervent prayers for the conversion of iniquitous Acre. Pedro Paixão was hardly troubled with the saintly ire of his wife, but came to town in his best *sakko* and stood dockside, the better to supervise the unloading of the feminine raw *matériel*.

Ideological Distension

Pedro Paixão began to change his thinking when that night, after dozing on the verandah while listening to the rain, he went in to lie down beside his wife and—manifesting a rare desire to fulfill his connubial obligations—caressed the firm thighs of Dona Vitória. In return, he received a painful lash from a rosary, across the hand, and an equally sharp tongue-lashing by his wife.

Conjugal Bed

DONA VITÓRIA: Look, you old lecherous goat, only after those degenerates have been thrown out of town. . . .

And with the bellow of a wounded beast, her husband repented a rosary that went on until morning.

A Comedy Worthy of Aristophanes

Pedro Paixão, days later, while having a beer in Puerto Alonso (his hand swathed in a melodramatic bandage), learned from several other landowners that there was a feminine complot afoot. And that Dona Vitória's act had political overtones. . . . Their women had apparently united to demand immediate expulsion of the "perverts" who were dominating Acre. And Paixão's friends, who added to these bedroom farces their own financial tragedies, were inclined to favor the total extirpation of my dissolute Empire. The situation called for urgent, decisive action, something that the common sense of Paixão was aptly suited for.

A General of the Future

Pedro Paixão pondered. The Empire had yet to be recognized by any government (he was dreaming of an ambassadorship in Europe; in Paris, to be exact). The price of rubber was plummeting and, to be perfectly honest, things were not turning out the way he had planned. It wasn't exactly pleasant to see those vagabond bands of *seringueiros*, drinking in every tavern in Puerto Alonso, idling like millionaires, when they should actually be producing such wealth.

The Conspirators

While we observed Christmas in my Palace with an unbridled orgy, Pedro Paixão was busy welcoming some of the more important plantation owners to his home at

Versailles. At the head of the table—not set for Christmas
supper, by the way, but bare and smoky for political cau-
cusing—sat Lieutenant Burlamaqui, in his impeccable uniform. The ironies of history: at the same table where,
months before, an empire had been planned (an empire
now in a pitiable state of decadence, I confess), a lieutenant
was offering his ready talents to put a quick end to the
reigning disorder.

The Proverbial Leader

Burlamaqui had long awaited an opportunity such as
this. It wasn't just anybody who could conceive the end
of a ruinous government and carry out his plan to per-
fection. He had many times felt a disdain for the Brazilian
government, with its inept and corrupt civilians, its fraud-
ulent politicians and venal bureaucrats. And all of them
rich, while he himself was obliged to lead the modest if
exemplary life of a soldier. Burlamaqui would minutely
plan every detail of the siege and fall of my Imperium, as
if it were but a model in miniature of some more ambitious
project of the future.

Password

The signal among the opposition for the launching of the
putsch would be: "Down with the cancan!" (An idea from
Dona Vitória.)

The Great Day

The 31st day of December arose splendidly. The sunlight was already illuminating the muddy streets, and the
docks had presented an unceasing flurry of activity since
early morning. Many had paddled for more than two days
to arrive, sleeping in their canoes under awnings of straw,
preparing their meals on small iron stoves. The harbor
was filled with such vessels—so oriental in appearance as
to lend the place an air of Chinese landscape about itself.

Along the main thoroughfare, the multitude awaited the start of the parade.

No one had slept that night at the Imperial Palace. We preferred to hold an intimate reception, eventually brought to a close by numerous toasts at six o'clock in the morning. So now I barely had time enough to take my bath and don my uniform of Field Marshal to a nonexistent Imperial Army; the outfit itself a fusion of Zouave and Hussar, confected by my French commandoes. Justine was elegantly attired, wearing a lovely blue dress and a gauze bonnet framing her hair in forget-me-nots *bien parisiens*. And there we were, the two of us, sweating hotly at the foot of the marble staircase to an as yet rather run-down Palace, where I was to cut the symbolic ribbon.

Unveiling

The marble staircase, prefabricated at the Lisbon School of Arts and Crafts for the price of seven hundred pounds, formed a bizarre combination with my storage-depot Palace. Its marble, streaked with pink, stood in awkward contrast to the muddy clapboard of Paixão's former property, and laughably malproportioned to its verandah of rusty zinc. The rise of majestic steps led nowhere, in one more metaphor of my Empire.

The Parade

It was an operatic vision of the history of Humanity. My subjects couldn't believe their eyes and stood petrified, watching. The Neanderthal men on palettes; Assyrians and Babylonians; Venus with Apollo, on an Olympus of paper; plus Caligula, Nero, Vercingetorix, Julius Caesar, and Napoleon; not to mention nomadic Berbers, nymphs with contours barely draped in toile, and tritons cresting on waves of blue satin. When the last allegorical float crossed the avenue, the people exploded in a wild burst of enthusiasm. Children danced, couples kissed, and grandparents cried. Nymphs, fauns, and historical figures fraternized with the masses . . . I saw a group of rubber workers carrying Napoleon in triumph.

THE EMPEROR OF THE AMAZON

Statistics

Effects of the celebration of the 31st day of December, 1899, in the city of Puerto Alonso: twenty cases of alcoholic coma resulting in death, two hundred cases of unwanted pregnancy, seventy cases of deflowerment, thirty-two divorces, eighty shotgun weddings, and ten disappearances. This, aside from my Empire itself, which was groaning. . . .

Réveillon

By nightfall, no one any longer knew anything and the alcohol had abolished all hierarchies. The interior of the Imperial Palace was a case in point, where visibly occupied bodies mutely exulted and ecstatic souls were lost in torrents of heat. . . . I know, but an orgy the likes of this one appeals to the latent Parnassian in me. Midnight was fast approaching, when the century would be capped by a spectacular pyrotechnical display. The racket was infernal, and viewed today, that New Year's gala seems to have been the final *danse macabre* of my ludicrous Empire.

Armed Might of an Empire

Moments before we were to begin the Royal Ball, Joana showed up with her Freedom Fighters, armed with rifles and carrying cases of ammunition. She ordered the Palace itself to be surrounded and had her men take up combat positions to defend my Imperium. In the twilight of a starlit evening, the Imperial Palace was quickly transformed into a fortress of pleasure. But I was not the slightest bit preoccupied with the fate of my regime.

The Siege of the Imperial Palace

The *coup d'état* commenced at nine at night, with an amphibious landing of counterrevolutionary troops. Burlamaqui organized a peremptory march to the Palace, collecting along the road the drunken and the dissolute, who were quickly tied up and hauled back to the warehouse nearest the dock. In front of the Palace itself, the counter-revolutionaries openly took up positions, then advanced as soon as Burlamaqui issued the cry of "Down with the cancan!" The Freedom Fighters at that point opened fire, and many of Burlamaqui's regulars fell dead. The initial panic would have turned into a rout, were it not for the coolheaded Burlamaqui, who began to shout his irritation and regroup his forces in the vicinity of the warehouse. Inside the Palace, several of us thought the new century was already being heralded in with explosions of fireworks, and we gave out with absurd salutations.

The Empire Defends Itself

Burlamaqui soon occupied all the houses surrounding the Palace and began to skirmish with the Freedom Fighters. Joana commanded her men with intelligence, returning fire only when it was possible to inflict some loss upon the counterrevolutionaries. The casualties, however, began to open holes in my ring of defense. Burlamaqui's men were becoming more and more daring, leaving the houses, crawling along the ground, taking advantage of the darkness.

The Fall of the Acrean Empire

The resistance of Joana's fighters was virtually liquidated within little more than an hour and a half. Of her thirty men, only nine escaped with their lives. And even these were seriously wounded. As the firing began to dissipate, Burlamaqui overran the barricades of rubber balls and stormed the Palace steps. The counterrevolutionaries fired into the air and shouted *vivas!* for Brazil.

Deposed

Burlamaqui entered the Palace and was struck by a wall of fetid heat and cigar smoke. He began searching for me, bent on the honor of deposing me personally. Ferreting his way through the confusion of drunkards, while ordering all the rooms to be summarily broken into, he encountered a number of memorable scenes. Blangis was arrested while bathing two nymphs with champagne, and Thaumaturgo Vaez while asleep on a sofa in my study, totally undressed and in the arms of the goddess Venus (a lovely Colombian, just in from Manaus). I was found lying unconscious amid a profusion of empty *jerez* bottles, protected by the darkness and isolation of the gazebo. Burlamaqui lifted me by the collar, and I offered no resistance. I opened my eyes with great difficulty, while down upon my head rained the shouts of the lieutenant. The bells of the church began to peal, announcing the twentieth century. In an effort to find a more comfortable position to meditate upon the event, I fumbled my way further into the arms of my deposer, but the exertion turned my stomach and, to my regret, I vomited copiously onto his uniform.

Heroine of the Nineteenth Century

I learned that Joana was shot down in the attempt to salvage my Empire. I lament and glorify her futile gesture. She fell dead on the steps of marble, and several threads of blood escaped from the eight bullet holes. Her Winchester beside her, still hot; her face encrusted with earth and blood. The lifted skirt offering one last glimpse of her tawny legs, which still seemed to throb, illuminated by the fireworks exploding across the sky.

The Logic of Memory

I was deposed by the twentieth century. A figure from the 1800s with no further immunities to the present, I have spent my last season in life with a few sheets of paper. And so we reach the end of my story, dear reader. My hands are tired and the agility is gone from my fingers. I am an old man who simply looks out upon a dazzle of arches and crispated minarets, among the salt mines of San Fernando, while appreciating the sweetness with which the sun warms

Cádiz. I lived, in the Amazon, the most intense moments of my whole existence and afterward marked time to my death. I, too, am a Spaniard of the melancholy generation.

Grand Finale ou Petite Apothéose

May the reader finally forgive me, but I have purloined the past from the gaiety of the memoir mixed with the intensity of the autobiography. I have rendered my adventures in the form they have always taken: a pastiche of serialized literature, the *feuilleton*—so minor, yet so rich with life. I have doled out my sensations among these chapters, and now I deliver my passing steps to an imaginary foot of the page in a *fin de siècle* newspaper.

Nature's Dialectic

Our hero existed in fact, exercising his nobility in the north of Brazil. He commanded one of the Acrean revolutions, and anyone who doubts the same may turn to a number of serious works to confirm our intimation. The picaresque moments in the life of Luiz Galvez wholly conform to the vaudevillian politics of the rubber boom. In a book by the scholar Veiga Simões, entitled *To This Side and That of the Sea*, published in Manaus, in 1917, by the Livraria Palais Royal, there is the following description of our hero:

> For a certain time, this audacious adventurer carried off the gesture that, later on, would bear repetition by Jacques Lebaudy, Emperor of the Sahara. Our Dom Galvez I, as long as he had the resources, did battle, led an army, and raised the flag of a new nation—as long as he had the resources. . . . Once they were depleted, his empire, like so many others, vanished into the abyss of all things picaresque, which leave the memory of themselves cloaked in ridicule. . . .

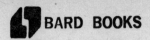 **BARD BOOKS**

DISTINGUISHED
LATIN-AMERICAN FICTION

THE AUTUMN OF THE PATRIARCH
Gabriel García Márquez   51300 2.95

BETRAYED BY RITA HAYWORTH
Manuel Puig   36020 2.25

DOM CASMURRO Machado De Assis   49668 2.95

DONA FLOR AND HER TWO HUSBANDS
Jorge Amado   35402 2.75

EPITAPH FOR A SMALL WINNER
Machado de Assis   33878 2.25

**THE EYE OF THE HEART: SHORT
STORIES FROM LATIN AMERICA**
Barbara Howes, Ed.   47787 2.95

GABRIELA, CLOVE AND CINNAMON
Jorge Amado   51839 3.95

THE GREEN HOUSE Mario Vargas Llosa   42747 2.25

HOPSCOTCH Julio Cortázar   36731 2.95

THE LOST STEPS Alejo Carpentier   46177 2.50

ONE HUNDRED YEARS OF SOLITUDE
Gabriel García Márquez   45278 2.95

SHEPHERDS OF THE NIGHT Jorge Amado   39990 2.95

TEREZA BATISTA
Jorge Amado   34645 2.95
